She Plus He Equals We

By: D'Ashanta

A Twisted Romance Standalone Novel

Dedications

First and foremost, I want to thank my Lord and Savior. Without you, I would be no one.

Mesha, you're an amazing publisher and friend. Thank you for cracking the whip on my ass and believing in me harder than most people I know.

Magnificent seven: Jap, Blac, Keedie, My Guy Ty, Big E, Bodie, and Kamster... words can't explain. Aside from being a part of the great eight, Jap you have been an amazing partner in all of this. I want you to know I am forever grateful to God and your family for blessing me with you.

Jade, you've been my bestie for a very long time. It's been times where you've had to talk me off the ledge and I am forever indebted to you for being selfless.

Christina, my wifey, you already know what it's hitting for. And for those of you who don't, you wouldn't understand, even if I explained. Love you my pretty.

Peezy, you've been one hunnit since we crossed paths in an author support group. I thank God for the chance introduction. If anyone were to look up the definition of "Day One" your beautiful picture is next to it.

TN, my author BAE. Thank you for always being there when I need you. The laughs, the votes of confidence, the drive you give me, and the random ass inbox questions you answer really does go a long way. I truly appreciate your genuine soul.

Fans, thank you for pushing me to the limits to stay in the game. We are definitely going places... see y'all at the top. God said, "Be patient."

In Memory Of:

Dontrell "Doc" Jackson	Stella Mae Riley
May 21, 1992 - December 7, 2015	October 20, 1953 - March 20, 2019

"If You Don't Remember Your Loved Ones Out Loud, They Die Twice."

Foreword from the Authoress

Hey My Shhhhshies,

First and foremost, thank you for your continuous support. The journey thus far has been a blessing to have you all ride with me as we witness growth, strength, and endurance. As I have been working hard to continuously pen books, I've also engaged in learning new ways to keep you all interested in my writings. One of the biggest tools I found was to be different. With that being said, this book is being released in the Romance genre because it's based off of love.

Knowing that I'm an atypical authoress, I'd like to forewarn my readers that there are very risqué scenes, more than the traditional amount of profanity, and an array of other R rated content. If any of these things are offensive to you, please DO NOT indulge.

If you are okay with the aforementioned warning, please grab your weapon of choice, a box of tissues, and find your favorite reading spot to enjoy your read. Thank you for downloading or purchasing the said title.

Be blessed,

Authoress D'Ashanta

Synopsis

Kenleigh Nguyen-Peters is a Blasian beauty who sees the good in everyone, is a Criminal Justice major with hopes of becoming the most sought out Private Investigator on her side of the Mississippi. Being raised by her father's twin brother and his wife, she's on a quest for clues to unanswered questions about her father's death and her mother's disappearance.

Struck by tragedy at a young age, Jawaine Franklin-Li, a young black man, was raised in the suburbs by his mother's best friend, Huang Li. After he'd buried his mom and had become a ward of the state, Huang felt responsible for his upbringing and stepped in to adopt him.

Jawaine watches from the sidelines as Kenleigh falls for the wrong guy. Although it hurts for him to watch, he sticks by her side to wipe her tears and mend her broken heart, because that's what best friends do. After they graduate college and go their separate ways, fate has it that their two ships pass in the night, ending up at the same dock.

Prologue

(Kenleigh's Perspective)

I sat here, wondering how my life got flipped upside down. It was like God wanted me to know where *He* stood because I went through every onslaught of hurt possible. The pain lasted several years, and I had taken a leap off the hypothetical ledge by losing myself in my husband's shadow. It had been years since I'd given up my identity to take on the role of the girlfriend and wife, becoming who he wanted me to be. However, when I'd finally decided to put me first, it was in that instance, I knew I needed to find myself again.

Had it not been for true love and chance encounters, I would perhaps be where my mother is. With everything I'd encountered, even I was surprised I hadn't committed murder. I was one pregnant side-bitch away from my very own episode of *Snapped*. Upon settling for what I thought was the love of my life, I found myself in situation after situation. Often, I would look at my worn reflection and ask, "Who the fuck did I marry?"

I'd graduated college, and the love of my life was drafted by the NFL during our second year of grad school, causing me to put my dreams on hold so I could be his ride or die. He both wanted and needed me to hold him down or so he'd said. We married a year after he was drafted, but I felt all I ever was, was his trophy.

He hated my best friend, and when I would tell most football wives that he did, their reaction was always the same, "Maybe they're fronting and are actually fucking?"

When I'd tell them, my best friend was a guy, they'd respond with a simple "Oh— "

Jawaine, my best friend, was accepted into an MBA program out in Milwaukee. I missed him so much. Our daily calls had turned into daily text, then turned into weekly text, then monthly. Now they were few, far, and between. He was the one who'd kept me grounded and my mental state in check.

The last verbal conversation we'd had, had resonated with me. He told me that he could no longer listen to me complain about the same shit that I'd been going through since our sophomore year of high school. He'd asked me what made me ever think Jonathan would change and if I was gonna continue to allow him to treat me this way, why was I complaining. After cussing him out like a dirty dog that pissed on my couch, he told me he loved me, and he'd keep me in his prayers. Everything between us had changed drastically that day. I moped around the house so badly that even Jon noticed, and he barely noticed anything.

Since then, my life had become an episode of Maury Povich, with me being the dumb bitch on the chair believing my husband could change his cheating ways. Five bastard ass love children and three fist fights with two of their mother's later, I found myself in Seattle, Washington attending a health and wealth conference, watching and listening attentively to my one true love who happened to be the keynote speaker.

I caught up to him afterward, we had dinner, then the two of us ended up back at my room at the Fairmont Olympic Hotel, catching up. There I sat, contemplating infidelity with my heart beating out of my chest. I'd barely found out I was pregnant with my husband's child and was a mess of emotions. Looking the love of my life in his eyes that were filled with adoration, I felt two ships had passed in the night, making all in the world right.

Passion-filled kisses, electrifying touches, and emotions that were undeniable had filled the gap that had been wedged between us so many years ago. Nevertheless, those same sentiments had me afraid. I hadn't been with anyone aside from my husband and the woman he'd practically forced me to share our bed with, during a threesome, on numerous occasions.

My head was spinning. Should I head for the hills, allowing my *one* to slip through the cracks yet again? Do I abort the child I'd longed for since the last of three previous miscarriages? Or do I tell *him* about my failed marriage, my plans to leave my husband, and how much this baby meant to me to see where it goes?

Four years ago...

Kenleigh Nguyen-Peters

Day 7,664:

Dear Diary,

I've searched the internet for what seemed like the millionth time. Still, nothing has returned under the name my adopted parents had given me for my estranged mother. Being raised by my uncle, who was my late father's twin, and his wife, I'd been afforded a great life. With all of that happening for me, it didn't negate the fact that I longed for more information on my background.

Dear Diary,

I need a backstory; I aspire to find my roots. My father was a very, handsome, melanin man. I vouch for that because he looked identical to Uncle Bucky being that they were identical twins, and my mother, well, it was my understanding that she was born Vietnamese. I had no vivid memories of either of them. From what I'd comprehended some years ago, my dad died in a car accident when I was seven months old and not much longer after that, my mother dropped me off to my dad's mother's house and disappeared.

I stood 5'6", had grey peepers hidden behind slanted eyelids, a small waist, and an apple bottom with hips as wide as a river's bend. Nah, I'm just kidding, but I took after my aunts who were triplets. They had hips and ass for days, but unfortunately, we hailed no boobs. God skipped us in that department. With that being said, I was barely a B cup.

Dear Diary,

You seem to get me off track worse than social media does with the social media trolls. Every time I write an entry, I tend to veer away from the subject at hand. Anyway, today was a productive day as far as classes went. I'm finally a third-year criminal justice student. Initially, I wanted to go to law school, but in pre-law, I decided to become a private investigator and invest in my own P.I. Firm.

For no reason other than wanting to get to the bottom of who I am, came that random decision. Who in the hell is Kenleigh Nightingale Nguyen-Peters? I'm more than a Blasian beauty with a small waist and a pudgy stomach, who happens to be in love with the man of my dreams, Jonathan Freeman. He was not only my man but everyone's guy because he was the star quarterback for our high school and now our college.

Dear Diary,

I know you have a plan for me, but what is it?

Ken

Riiiiiiing!

The buzzer rang, alerting us that class was out. I finished writing my daily entry, snatched my journal from the desk, and with my luck, my pen flew in the opposite direction. As it happens, the pen hit one of Jonathan's groupies on the leg. She also happened to be the captain of the cheer squad.

"Hey bum, what the hell is your problem?" Jamaica's fake lash fluttering lookers shot daggers into my direction as she waited for a response.

"Um, it was an accident." I marched over to retrieve my pen. Unfortunately, she was surrounded by her group of flunkies, also known as the cheer co-captain and a few of the cheerleaders. One of whom had grabbed my pen before I'd made it to where it had fallen.

"Um, it was an accident," LaShay, the co-captain teased, attempting to mock me. "If it was such a fuckin' accident, apologize to our team captain so you can get this cheap ass pen back."

"Gang, gang," Johneisha, another of the cheerleaders tuned in.

Johneisha and I were once best friends throughout grade school up until our freshman year of high school. Then she formed an alliance with the Mean Girls crew and was banished from ever talking to me again.

"Well, actually, the pen isn't cheap. The package of four Uniball Vision Elite's costs twelve bucks, so you're holding a three-dollar pen. May I please have it back?" I asked her Messy Mya looking ass. May he rest in peace. He was a social media comedian who was killed before he had a chance to blow up. He was beautiful. However, she looked like a man.

Extending her hand, she rapidly took it back, slammed the pen on the floor, then stomped on it. In doing so, the pen shattered, causing the ink to splatter onto Jamaica's white skinny jeans. They looked to be both expensive and new.

The look on Jamaica's face was priceless, but the look on LaShay's face was that of a scared puppy.

"What the fuck, LaShay? These jeans were $220, so I'm gonna need that by the end of the business day, today," Jamaica demanded.

LaShay's parents were blue-collar, but they weren't cashing out like Aunt Junie and Uncle Bucky. Aunt Junie owned several beauty supply stores, and Uncle

Bucky had his own bounty hunting and process serving business. Any time you saw him coming, it wasn't good.

"Ha, ha, ha. When you do dirt, karma comes back for you," I taunted. Spinning on my heels, I started to walk off.

I was stopped dead in my tracks as my head was yanked back by my curly ponytail. The one time I wore my real hair out, I was pulled by it. I typically wore a clip-on pony that looked similar to the hair God had blessed me with. I wasn't a scrapper, but I wasn't afraid to fight, LaShay snuck me though. Before either of us got a chance to swing, Jawaine walked up and broke us up. Where he'd come from, I had no idea. What I did know, was he saved her from an ass-whooping.

Jawaine was my neighbor. I met him when the Li's adopted him. What a world we lived in? Here I was, half Asian, raised by my aunt and uncle, and Jawaine was black, raised by Asians. He was my best friend since third grade. When the girls crooned over how fine he was, standing at six-foot-three with broad shoulders, hazel eyes, and pecks for days, all I was the scrawny, little, pissy tail boy I grew up with... ewe!

Walking into my next class, I noticed my best friend Kenleigh about to get down with one of the cheerleaders. I knew things were gonna get ugly because they didn't fight fair. They fought dirty because none of them were scrappers. The only time I had ever witnessed any of them win a fight, was when two of the others held the opponent down.

"Hey, what the hell is going on?" I pushed between the ladies to free Kenleigh's hair from LaShay's tight grasp.

"She in here talking shit like she bad. Let her get her ass whooped like she bad."

"Is it really over her talking shit, or are you still mad that she was chosen, and you were only good enough to be a jump-off?"

"Tuh, trick, please. I ain't nobody's jump-off." LaShay waved me off. Judging by her facial expression, it seemed like I had outed her.

"So, I didn't see Jay creeping out of your window Sunday morning before your parents pulled in from their business trip?" I said, allowing my petty to run as deep as hers.

"Bish, whet? So, you mean to tell me you're slaying John behind my back?" Jamaica pushed LaShay's shoulder. "You better have my money for my jeans. Otherwise, I'm fucking you up on sight. One for messing up my jeans and two for messing with my man behind my back."

Snap. Snap.

At the snap of her fingers, the rest of Jamaica's flunkies filed in; one grabbed her handbag, and the other grabbed her laptop bag, then followed behind her like lovesick puppies.

"I hate you, Jawaine, with your messy ass. I bet you gay. I mean what other excuse do you have to be so petty and what dude has a female best friend?" LaShay cried.

"I bet I get more snatch than you get pipe being that you're sharing with your 'best friend.'" I ruminated. She was speechless and had a look of discernment on her face. "Oh, ok. That's exactly what I thought. Let's go, KeKe. Fuck she thought this was?"

"Why did you have to be so mean to her?" KeKe quizzed as we ambled toward the exit.

"Don't nobody fuck with my best friend. If they come for you, they get us. We a team," I reiterated.

Kenleigh was sexy as hell, but I would never cross the line with her because I loved our friendship. I could tell her anything and not be judged, as she could me. She had only been with one dude, I think. I thought he was unworthy, but who was I to hate on either of them? On the same note and in the same tune, if she ever wanted me to kick his ass, I would, in a heartbeat.

"Why are you always so protective of me? I don't deserve you, Wanky." She locked her tiny arm around mine and leaned her head on my shoulder as we strutted down the hallway.

I escorted her to her car to ensure her safety and then headed back to class. Of course, I was late, but who was gonna check me? Sitting in my seat, I yawned while the professor did his lecture, and uninterestedly doodled on notebook paper. Being a criminal justice major, my endgame was to become a detective. My parents were murdered in cold blood in front of me when I was six. It was a vivid memory that would haunt me until I found the motherfucker that did it. I'd never forgotten his face or his voice.

"I'm about to slide through," I voiced to a distraught Kenleigh.

Her sniffles made me want to kill every man walking as I made my way to my awaiting 2018 black on silver Mazda 6. I felt indifferent for the way I'd gotten dressed and ran off, leaving one of my sex buddies hot and naked, but KeKe needed me. Whenever she called, I would drop everything and run to her aid.

As I jumped in and headed towards Kenleigh's house, I decided to clear the air and change my aura by listening to music. I tuned into Kevin Gates' *Satellites* and calmed my nerves. Driving along while rapping the lyrics, my phone rang through the Bluetooth, interrupting the one-man show. Deciding to answer, I swiped my finger along the arrow.

"What's good?"

"Don't what's good me, Jawaine. What in the hell is wrong with you? You got out of my yoni and left without any explanation," my lil snow bunny, yelled.

"Listen, Heather, don't call me with that good bullshit. I'm single, and I don't report to no fuckin' body."

I had to calm myself because I was roughly ten seconds away from verbally handing her ass to her and not thinking twice about it.

"I'm sorry, I didn't mean anything by it. It's just that you left so abruptly, and didn't call to say anything, so I was concerned, baby," she whined.

I bet she was sorry. The kid didn't have time to play mind games with her or anyone. I was a junior in college, young, dumb, and full of cum. A brother had ambitions and dreams, none of which allowed time for a girlfriend. I told females from the beginning what it was, and that was sex. At that moment, it could be with her, her, or her. Being that I was completely transparent, I wanted to think they wouldn't have any misunderstandings and wouldn't get anything between us misconstrued. Apparently not, because look at the shit popping between me and Heather.

"Well, I'll accept your apology—this time. But look, don't ever in your life come at me sideways again."

"I'm sorry, Daddy. Are you gonna come back over? My roommate is gone out of town with her boyfriend for the weekend," she cooed. "No one's here besides me and Jokester."

Jokester was her fish. It was the coolest looking beta fish I'd ever seen. He also had an intriguing personality. Every time I'd walk up to the oversized tank and put my hand on the glass, he'd swim over to it extremely fast as if he was trying to scare me off.

"Yeah, well I have no idea if I'm gonna make it back or not. I'm not sure what's going on, but I had an emergency, and I'm gonna tend to it, so I'll talk at ya later."

"I bet you do have an emergency. I'm pretty sure that only person that called you with such an emergency was that bitch, Kenleigh. No matter what we're doing, when *she* calls, you run off like *her* little puppy. You always leave for *her*," she spat, her tone laced in envy.

"See, this is the type of shit I don't have time for," I voiced.

With that, I disconnected the phone call. I did not play games with these females when it came to be being disrespectful to or about my releationship Kenleigh.

Pulling up to Kenleigh's residence, I noticed her sitting on the free swing that her aunt had built back when we were in tenth grade. She looked so broken, I just wanted to fix her. I wish I could take away all her pain. I felt like the song, *If I Could* by Regina Belle. If I could, I would protect her from the sadness in her eyes. I would protect her from the world of great big compromise. I would if I could.

"So, Jon was kicking it with LaShay," I admitted in embarrassment.

"Okay?" Jawaine sat there with a blank expression on his face.

"Okay? This is devastating. He told me he was gonna see who he damn well pleased because I was still holding out on the goods."

"Your goods? Wait!? You're still holding onto your V-Card?" Jay laughed in amusement.

"It's not funny." I giggled lightly. "I lied about giving it up because I thought it was cool at the time. Shut up!"

"Bruh, that shit hurt," he complained.

I'd punched his arm for laughing but joined in at my own expense. I was genuinely hurt by Jon and LaShay being sexual with one another. However, when Jawaine was around, I couldn't stay sad or upset for very long.

"Listen, if you keep allowing this dude to run all over you, that's all he'll ever do because that's what he's used to. If you don't hold him accountable for his actions, what do you think will change?"

"Why are you always so judgmental of him. You're supposed to support me, regardless," I yelled.

I was no longer interested in laughing with him. He was tap dancing on my patience.

"Really, KeKe? You think I'mma support this farce of a relationship, regardless? You're sadder than you're happy when it comes to what you and Jon have or don't have. You been dealing with dude since tenth grade, and now you're a junior in college, and you haven't genuinely smiled in most of the years he's been your boyfriend. Every time you call me crying, it's about him and what he's done."

"It is not, and you know it."

"It is too, KeKe. Stop being so naïve. He's not the only man on earth and he damn sure isn't deserving. Being the 'main chick' of the star quarterback shouldn't be enough! You should demand more than a title, love."

"It's easy for you to say. You're popular with the opposite sex. You're smart, you apparently have sex appeal, and all the above. The girls seem to think you're a great catch."

"What say you? Who thinks I'm a great catch?" Jawaine half-smiled.

"Really? Is that the only thing you've heard the whole time I've been talking?"

"Nope, I heard everything. The only thing that concerns me is that you need to leave the fuck boy before you give him what he doesn't deserve, KeKe."

"What's that?"

"Your virginity. You can't believe he deserves your all or am I reaching when I assume that you think that'll make him change his set ways?"

"I knew I shouldn't have told you that he never had the cookie."

"Is that right?"

"Yeah. You don't care about nothing besides me keeping my virginity and who thinks you're a great catch." I tried to skate right through the fact that he mentioned me not giving up the goods...for a second time.

When Jon told me that he was having sex with other females because I wouldn't have sex with him, I decided to go ahead and give it up to him so I could keep him satisfied. I planned on getting it on and popping later. If I told Jawaine what I was planning to do, he wouldn't let me live it down because he thinks he knows every God forsaken thing. I loved him as a best friend and wished Jon possessed some of his qualities, such as treating me like a woman rather than a jump-off or side piece. Unfortunately, that wasn't the case. Jon was my man, and Waine was my bestie.

I'd already packed my overnight bag and was waiting for Jon to pick me up. After our very public argument, he stormed off, pissed, and I texted him to pick me up later. Deciding to book a room at the DoubleTree Hotel, I pulled out all the stops that I imagined I needed to lose my virginity.

"Hellooooo? Kenleigh, are you listening? Have you heard a damn word I said in the last five minutes?"

"Yeah, I heard you. Sheesh," I breathed.

I sure hoped he didn't ask me to repeat anything.

"Ok then, I'll holla atcha," Jawaine stood to his feet, and outstretched his never-ending arms, then leaned his head to the left side.

Standing to my feet, I stepped up to him and hugged him like we'd never see each other again. He kissed the top of my head innocently, then turned to head to his car. Something about the kiss he placed on my head felt different. I wasn't sure what was going on internally, but I was now questioning if I should follow through with the plans I'd aforementioned.

Before Jawaine was off the porch good, Jon whipped into his normal spot at the curbside. The tension between them could be cut with a knife. At times, I thought it was because of me, and other times, I thought it was just an ego thing between two-star football players.

"What's up, Jay? Why you got ya trifling ass lips all over my woman?" Jon yelled in Jay's face after they'd approached one another on the sidewalk.

"Bruh, don't come at me about shit I do with my best friend. I been in her life, nigga. You barely know what she likes and dislikes."

"I know she like this dick. This is my bitch, and you or no one else is gon' come between us." Jon seethed in absolute anger.

Apparently, he'd been drinking. His eye was glossed over, and his demeanor was a bit scary. I had never seen him this way before, and we'd been dating for five years. He shoulder-bumped Jawaine as he brushed past him. Why did he have to do that? Jawaine didn't play when his personal space was violated. When he turned around to face Jon, I decided to intervene.

"Jon, I can promise you this ain't what the fuck you want my nigga."

"Oh, you use that type of language with Asian parents. You best get ya bitch ass on before you get what you looking for my boy."

"And what's that my nigga? Don't threaten me with a good time. I been waiting for a moment to dance with you. Let's goooo!"

"Please, guys stop this foolishness. What are you doing, you're teammates? Is that not enough common ground for the two of you to squash whatever beef y'all have?" I stood amid the two on the makeshift battlefield, looking between the men.

"Nah, whatever the fuck he wanna do, let us do it. You need to play your part and stay outta grown man shit," Jon gritted as he pulled me to the side. His grip was a bit tight, but I didn't say anything, afraid of further upsetting him.

No sooner than Jon released my arm, Jawaine's fist connected with his jaw. From there, they were scuffling on the front lawn with me, screaming to the top of my lungs for them to stop fighting. The neighbors had come out along with my Aunt Junie and Uncle Bucky.

"Hey, you heathens break it up, now," Aunt Junie yelled.

Them ignoring her pleas obviously pissed my uncle Bucky off to the fullest. He pulled a huge gun from the holster on his hip and cocked the hammer back. It was then they decided to cease their animalistic ways.

"Now, someone tell me why the hell you two are at each other's throats," Uncle Bucky demanded.

"I pulled up to pick my girl up, and this ni–, dude was kissing all on the top of her head like she's his girl or something," Jon stated with angst.

He'd corrected his language, knowing that my uncle despised ratchetness.

"Nah, that's not what happened. He's been holding a grudge since middle school. I took his girl to the eighth-grade prom, and he's been on one since. The reason I stole him tonight though, Unc, is because he referred to Kenleigh *his bitch* instead of *his lady* or *his girl* and he grabbed her by the arm."

"Kenleigh, is that what happened?" Uncle Bucky queried with rage in his eyes.

"Uncle Bucky, it wasn't like Jawaine's making it out to be. He's overexaggerating per usual. Jon told him to keep his lips off me after he'd witnessed Jay innocently kiss the top of my head as he's done all of our lives. Then, I got between them to try and stop the childish quarrel from going any further when Jon grabbed my arm to move me out of the way. That was it," I ogled Jay with intensity.

"If this Q & A session is over, Kenleigh, I would like to be excused. We have a date tonight."

Uncle Bucky looked disappointed, yet he moved to the side while motioning his hand in a 'floor is yours' manner. I went inside and grabbed my large Michael Kors bag, then headed back outside to Jon's car where he waited.

"Leigh," my aunt called out.

"Ma'am?"

"Be careful with that one, baby girl," she hugged and kissed me on the cheek.

I couldn't believe my ears. Kenleigh stood there and sided with the bastard of the night. I wanted to slap the smirk right off his community dick having ass face. I couldn't believe he had her nose wide open to the point where she accepted all of his bullshit. Hopping in my car, I decided to smash out and head back over to Heather's place. Bobbing my head to the music, I rapped along with Kevin Gates.

"She special to you

I don't look at her special

Actually, I treat her regular

Not being seen, we not making no spectacle

Gates had her first, then he gave her to Kevin."

As the lyrics to *Really, Really* rolled off my tongue, I realized I was caught up in a situation with my best friend and her dude because of feelings she didn't know existed. I cared about her deeply, but for the life of me, I couldn't figure out why my feelings were on the brim of love when she'd never given me more than a friendship to assume anything more could come of us.

After whipping my car into the spot that I'd been in before leaving earlier, I hopped out. Taking the stairs two by two, I made it up to her door, ready to dive into her juice box with aggression.

Knock. Knock.

I waited for her to respond. After a few seconds had passed, I'd decided to knock again. Moments later, I heard giggling and a male voice on the other side. Heather opened the door, enveloped in a silk bedsheet.

"Oh, my bad. I had no idea you had company," I voiced.

"Yeah, she does. But can we help you, though?" The male expressed over her shoulder, startling her.

"Nah, son. Neither of you can help me. I'm good."

With the tidbit of information presented before me, I spun on my heels to beat my feet. There was no reason to be upset or surprised. I gotta be honest with myself because just like me, Heather was single and free to have sex with whomever she chose. It was my bad that I showed up to her place without calling first.

It was mid-May and a Friday night. I knew there had to be something to get into. Deciding to drive around campus housing looking for a party, I found just what I was looking for. It was just my luck. It seemed the Kappa Alpha Psi fraternity was having a party. With that came Alpha Kappa Alpha sorority chicks. I was definitely down for that type of party. They were the so-called pretty ones amongst all sororities, but they were the freaks, and they absolutely had no holds barred when it came to athletes.

After parking my car, I jumped out that thang and was immediately recognized by males and females. Walking through the crowd, daps and hugs were given freely. I looked to my right and noticed Kenleigh standing around, holding hands with Jon. Everything in me wanted to go knock that nigga on his ass, but I decided to let him live.

The way Kenleigh stood thereof to the side of the front door, looking lost while he whispered in a soror's ear made me feel uneasy. The soror stood with an ingenuine smile on her face, but that meant nothing. After what KeKe had done earlier today, I decided to keep my distance because I didn't want any more drama. I wanted to get full, have a great time, and fall off in some new coochie.

Approaching the front door unnoticed by either of them, had almost gone successfully. Had it not been for Biansha, the girl who's ear Jon was whispering in, I may have made it.

"Hey Jawaine," she sang out in a melodic tone.

"What's good, love?"

"Damn, you just gon' keep walking. I'm trying to holla at you, boo."

"Come talk to me then, sexy." I reached my hand out.

Never missing a beat, she brushed past Jon, giving Kenleigh a sympathetic glare, and grabbed ahold of my hand. As we walked into the Frat house, I looked over my shoulder and into the very upset face of Jon. *The fuck he upset for. He's with his girl.* I thought to myself.

"What's up with you?" Biansha inquired.

"Not much, love. I was just passing through and noticed the party, so I stopped to see what was popping. What's crackin' with you?"

"Nothing really. I allowed my line sisters to get me outta the dorm tonight," she rubbed my arm. "Your boy, Jon, is a trip," she informed me as we took a seat on the leather loveseat.

"Why you say that?" I queried.

She shook her head, fervently. "Can you believe he had his girlfriend's hand in his and was still trying to hook up with me after he drops her off back home tonight?"

"Wow! That's some pussy shit."

"That poor girl. She had to pretend not to hear him because I'm sure he spoke loud enough for her to overhear his so-called whisper."

"Yeah, that's pretty pathetic on both their parts. Enough about them, though. You wanna grab something to drink?"

"I don't drink," she shrugged. "But I'll go grab one for you if you'd like," Biansha offered.

"Yeah, that'll be nice," I looked at her.

"What?"

"Don't put no date rape drug in my shit."

It was like I'd told the absolute funniest joke she'd ever heard. But when she saw that I wasn't laughing she stopped. As quick as she stopped laughing, I cracked up. I laughed so hard I had tears in my eyes.

"You should've seen your face when I didn't engage."

"Nah, you know what, you can go get your own shit," she pouted.

It was cute. I was absolutely surprised that she didn't drink. Being at a frat party, it was like a prerequisite to be a drinker or a smoker or even a pill head. But whatever, I guess.

"That's fine. Don't let nobody slide in my spot while I'm gone. That is if it's still my spot since you can't take a joke and all."

"It depends… if he's as intelligent, as tall, and as handsome as you are, he might have a chance." She smiled.

I headed in the direction of the kitchen. Of course, it was bodies throughout the pathway, some dancing, some receiving head, some in the middle of sexual activity, and some merely talking. Grabbing a cup and filling it with Jungle Juice, and because I was raised correctly, I decided to take a bottle of Core water back for Biansha. The taste of the concoction in the cup had me feeling good already.

"Here you go, love."

"You didn't spike it with a date rape drug, did you?" she smiled which onset my half-grin.

"Here you go. Is this what we're gonna do the rest of the night?"

"Nope, just until I'm tired enough to go home."

"Home? Who said you were going home?"

"Uh, me. I have to make-up a test tomorrow at eleven. It's almost one, so I'll be getting outta here soon."

"Let's go for a ride, Biansha," I suggested, deciding to shoot my shot.

"I'll go on two conditions."

"And they are?"

"You promise to have me home by 2:30 and you don't try none of that nasty shit. My granny always said nothing was open this late at night but motels and legs. Although I think you're sexy, I'm not that kind of girl."

"I don't follow."

"Oh, you follow. But since you wanna play dumb, I'mma let you know what it's hitting for."

"What's that?"

"C'mere," she grabbed me by the shirt, pulling me to her until my ear was near her mouth. "I don't fuck on the first, second, or third date," she kissed my cheek before releasing my shirt.

I lifted my head, stood to my feet, and outstretched my hand for Biansha to grab. As she stood, I looked directly into the faces of Kenleigh and Jon.

A few weeks had passed, and Biansha and I were forming a great friendship. As per mentioned the night of the party, she did not have sex with me on the first, second, or third date. Hell, the fourth or fifth one either. School was finally out. However, she'd chosen to take summer classes so she could walk with the May graduates rather than the following December.

I pulled up to the same spot I'd dropped her off in this morning since all of her classes were in the same hall. Ninny came walking out, looking like a whole meal. Don't get me wrong, she wasn't the most beautiful that I'd been with nor was she the sexiest. She was top heavy with no ass. On top of that, she had a green eye and a grey eye with light brown skin. Sometimes she'd put a contact in either eye to make the colors match, but for the most part, she was comfortable with it because it was something she'd lived with her whole life. Nonethelss, her sex appeal was undeniable. I couldn't understand why I'd been so horny lately. I mean I got head from Heather a few times.

I learned over time that Biansha's name was actually supposed to be Bianka. Rumor has it that her mother was so high on drugs that she couldn't write worth a damn, and what she'd written was illegible. However, her family and friends referred to her as Ninny. Her granny nicknamed her that because her father spoiled her and the moment, she didn't get her way, she'd whine until she did. I hadn't experienced that side of her… yet.

"Hey baby," she smiled as she sat in the passenger seat.

"What's up? How was class, boo?"

"It was class. You know how they cram four months of lessons into two months. I didn't think about how fast-tracked it would be. But, I'm not a failure so I will thrive, and I will pass these classes, standing on my head." She kissed my lips, then buckled her seatbelt.

"That's my baby! You hungry?"

"I can definitely eat."

"Good cuz I made us reservations at Benihana."

"Really," she squealed.

"Yeah, we got thirty minutes to get there. You've been working hard in class. Plus, you said you've never been, so—why not?" I shrugged.

She snatched me by the shirt and pecked my lips several times. She was very appreciative of any and everything I did for her. I pulled off into the direction of the restaurant, and my phone began to ring, interrupting J. Cole's *Crooked Smile*. I looked at the screen and saw that it was Kenleigh. It was probably nothing, so I ignored it. To no avail, she called right back.

"Yeah?"

"I need to talk to you," she cried.

"Do you need me to come right away?"

"Yeah, I do Jawaine."

"Okay, but I don't have much time."

"I just need a few minutes to talk, please."

Disconnecting the line, I looked over at Ninny with questioning eyes. She half-smiled and nodded her head, giving me the okay to go to my best friend's aid. I explained the nature of our friendship to her on our third date. Thankfully, we had to pass our neighborhood to get to the restaurant.

Minutes later, I parked my car on the curb, not bothering to cut the engine. There sat Kenleigh, looking as pathetic as she usually did when she allowed the fuck boy to fuck over her. I walked up to her, and she stood to hug me, but I gave her a half-ass hug that she noticed.

"What's wrong with you and why didn't you turn your car off?"

"My girl is in the car. I can't leave her in there without A/C at the beginning of July. What's up KeKe?" I breathed. I wasn't feeling it.

"Can you go drop her off and come back. I need my best friend."

"Nope, we have plans."

"Nope? Plans?"

"Yeah," I voiced. "You're living your life undisturbed with the loser of the century. Am I supposed to be at your beck and call for the rest of my life? You must've bumped your head, Kenleigh."

The passenger's door opened and out stepped Ninny. A smile graced my face. My baby was nice. Even with all her flaws, her poise, intelligence, and the simple yet complex conversation we held with one another made her sexy as fuck to me.

"Baby, we have twenty minutes to make our reservation time. Do you want me to call and cancel?" Ninny queried, innocently.

"Baby? Reservation?"

Kenleigh reminded me of the Soulja Boy interview when he said, "Drake? Tyga?" I couldn't help but contain my laughter.

"Nah, here I come, love," I responded. After she'd gotten back in the car, I answered Kenleigh. "Yeah, baby and yeah, reservation."

"So, are you two dating now?"

"Kenleigh, why does it matter? You've been so high-strung on Jon that you haven't noticed me or the changes I've made over the last few weeks." I sighed. "Do you wanna tell me what's going on or not? I got five minutes."

"No, you can go with your *baby* or whatever," she spat, her tone laced in what I'd assumed to be jealousy.

"Oh, I see what this is. Nah, not this time, KeKe. I'm no longer putting you before me. The more of me I give you, the less of me I have."

Outstretching my arms, Kenleigh refused to stand to her feet to embrace me in a hug. Not in the mood to allow her to cloud my judgment, I leaned over and kissed the top of her head. Jogging the length of the sidewalk to my car, I hopped in the driver's seat, then headed to the restaurant.

Seventeen months later…

Kenleigh

"Leigh, I can't tell you how proud of you I am, Sugar Bear," my aunt Junie boasted, boosting my confidence.

It was finally graduation day. Undergrad was a mess. I'd grown from a girl to a woman. A young woman, but a woman, nonetheless. I looked around at all the grads.

"Where's Uncle Bucky?"

"He went to visit Kenny Lee's gravesite. You know he shares each monumental moment in your life with your dad."

"I didn't realize he did until this very moment. That explains why he's always right on time for everything."

"Yep, that would be the reason. He should be here before the commencement starts, even if he doesn't, you're in the N's so he has plenty of time to make it to see you walk."

"Aunt Junie, can you believe I did it? I'm graduating from college!" Jawaine picked my aunt up and spun her around while his mother, my play aunt, stood back, smiling.

"Put me down, silly ass child." She laughed. "Where's that beautiful girlfriend of yours?"

"She's down the hall with her family and friends."

"I can't believe he's finally settled down. I thought his pecker would be near falling off before he did," aunt Huang chimed in, causing me to roll my eyes.

"What was that, Leigh?" my aunt questioned.

"What was what, Aunt Junie?"

"I'm not about to play with you."

"Where's Jon?" Aunt Huang queried.

"Who knows?" My aunt mumbled, but it was audible enough for us all to understand.

"Aunt Junie, really?"

"Well, she only said what you were thinking. It was obvious by your facial expression. Either way, I saw him down there, giving congratulations to the cheer squad, specifically LaShay." Jawaine butted in with his two cents. "I'm sure he'll be here to congratulate you shortly." His eyebrow raised questionably.

We stood around, talking for a few more minutes before we filed into the auditorium to take our seats. As I approached the foyer to take my place in line, I noticed Jon and LaShay swapping spit behind a pillar. They hugged lovingly before he ran to line up with his group. Being that his last name started with an F, he had to line up in front of both me and Jawaine.

I felt so stupid, here it was over a year since I gave him my virginity, which was the worst possible experience I'd ever had, and he was still fucking everything that had a pussy. How could I be so dumb? Now that I'm addicted to his love, I felt like I was even more naïve than what I was to begin with. Looking straight ahead, I noticed Jawaine ogling me with empathy-filled orbs.

LaShay brushed past me, nearly bumping my shoulder, but I didn't allow her to because I stepped aside, knowing that today would've been the day she got her ass stomped out. I wasn't feeling what I'd just witnessed, and it was messed up that everyone around me had also been privy to the same encounter. He was supposed to be my boyfriend, yet there he stood, publicly humiliating me in the presence of our family, friends, and classmates.

Just as tears filled my ducts, someone walked in with a huge bouquet of flowers, balloons, and signs with Jawaine and my photos printed on either side of them.

"What's up, Uncle Bucky? You did it big, huh, old dude!" Jawaine stepped out of the line to dap and hug my uncle.

"I sure did. Tell me any other way to do it, and I'll handle that for graduation from the master's program."

You'd think Jawaine was his nephew, and I was the neighbor the way the two of them got along. My uncle was not very fond of Jon, and after witnessing what I had today, I knew the hunch he'd warned me of at the beginning of Jon and my relationship, was right. He wasn't any good for me but like Mary J. Blige said in the *Mr. Wrong* song she has with Drake… I love my mister wrong.

After they finished chopping it up, Uncle Bucky took notice of me and headed my way. I stood holding my breath and smiling forcefully because I didn't want him to catch wind of my ill feelings.

"Hey, Sugar Bear," he kissed my temple. "Are you excited?"

"Yes, I'm stoked, Uncle. I never thought I'd see the day I walked across the stage to receive my degree in criminal justice.

"That's right, baby girl, I'll be the loudest mothersucker in the auditorium. Don't be embarrassed like you were at your high school graduation. I'm so proud of you."

My uncle hugged me tightly. It was as if he knew I needed to feel his love at the very moment. In his arms, the world was a safe place. I wasn't privy to heartache, pain, or any evil. Once he released me, the tears flowed freely. I was overwhelmed by everything going on.

"Hey Mr. Peters, that's a nice setup you got there. You sholly do come through with the clutch when it come to Kenleigh," I heard LaShay. Her last name was Nunnery, so she was mere feet from me.

"Come through with the what? Speak English, child," Uncle Bucky responded.

I almost choked on the spit I swallowed. He knew what she meant, but again, he didn't like ratchetness. He was a man full of education and articulation. He spoke to people, not at people, and he annunciated every syllable. He was raised by two professors. My grandmother was an English professor here at the University of Alabama, and my grandfather was a Philosophy professor at Auburn. Two rivals had an undying love for one another.

Their love story was like Allie and Noah's. The only difference is my grandmother passed after my grandfather did. It was so sad. Paw-Paw died February 13, 2001, and Gran-Gran passed February 15, 2001. My uncle Bucky, and my aunts Misha, Tisha, and Gisha, decided to put them side by side in a mausoleum rather than bury them in the ground.

"What I mean is, every time Kenleigh has a function, you go all out for her."

"I sure do. Every accomplishment is to be celebrated. Where are your parents?"

"They're on a business trip, per usual," LaShay responded sadly.

"This is more important than business. Couldn't they change their business plans in order to see their only child walk across the stage? This is monumental. Money is ever-flowing, time is not. The memories created tonight will last a lifetime." He seethed.

"Bucky, that's enough," my aunt Junie pulled him away.

She wanted to stop him before he went too far, but from the looks of things, he'd already gotten LaShay in her feelings. Even with everything she'd been doing with my boyfriend behind my back, I wanted to hug her and tell her everything would be alright. I didn't understand why she would want to be someone's side chick, but I guess with her parents always out of the country, she lacked guidance. My heart went out to her.

We filed into the auditorium and were seated as rehearsed. During the commencement, there were several keynote speakers from recent alumni to twenty-year alumni. It was pretty dope, to say the least. A choir came in and sang a song for the graduates. Flyers were being passed around during our exit. Unbeknownst to me, Uncle Bucky had arranged a party for the graduates at a nearby reception hall.

After going home and getting changed, I met up with Jawaine at his house to see if he'd be attending the function. I hadn't seen or talked to him much since the night he'd had a fight with Jon. I mean truthfully, I had taken sides when I usually stayed out of it. I didn't want either of them pissed with me. However, I knew it would be easier to get Jay back in my good graces than it would've been to reel Jon in.

"Jawaine, are you going to the graduation party?" I asked after walking into the house and into his room.

"Yeah, me and my girl gon' slide through."

"Can you put some clothes on. though?" I laughed.

"Nah, I just got out the shower, and you walked into *my* room without knocking on *my* door. A few minutes earlier and you would've caught an eyeful of all of my glory," he laid back on the chair near the window in his room.

"Ugh. I don't wanna see that. Your print is busting through the towel, so it's not doing you any justice."

Inside I screamed. I knew for sure his package was bigger than Jon's just by looking at it. I had never seen the sex appeal he exuded before today. Damn, Jawaine was tall, dark, and handsome. His teeth were slightly gapped, and the scar on his upper lip from the cleft surgery was barely noticeable. He'd had a few corrective surgeries to fix it. I felt my pussy getting wet with just my imagination.

"What's wrong with you, KeKe?"

"What? Huh? What you mean?"

"If I didn't know any better, I'd assume you were standing there, lusting over this meat pack." He made his dick rise and fall twice.

"Nah, ewe! No one wants you, Jawaine. You're like my brother, and that's gross!" I curled my lip in a disgusted manner.

"Uh huh, that's what your mouth says, but your headlights are on high beam." He grinned.

"How do you know? You can't see my car from here."

"Girl, ain't nobody talking about no damn car. Ha, ha!" he laughed and glowered at my boobs.

"Oh my God, you're so nasty. I'm out, I'll see you at the party," I stammered.

Flustered, I got out of there before I did something I'd later regret. If I said that Jawaine didn't look like a box of my favorite Godiva chocolates, I'd be lying.

That boy looked scrumptious. I now understood what females meant when they said a man looked so good, they could eat them up.

Opening the door, Biansha stood there in motion to ring the doorbell.

"Congrats on your graduation," she smiled.

"Yeah, you too." I half-smiled.

Saying that I wasn't jealous that she'd taken my best friend away from me would be an understatement. Seeing what was wrapped in the towel, I definitely understood why she'd locked him down.

Now she wants to see a nigga. Nah, she doesn't get to do that. I sat in the chair still wrapped in the towel that donned my waistline, covering up my junk. Smiling at what had just happened, I was interrupted by someone clearing their throat.

"Hey baby," I spoke as Ninny stood at my room door, looking crazy as hell.

"Hey baby? What's this?"

"I just got out of the shower." I raised my eyebrow in confusion.

"Jawaine, you can't think I'm stupid. I know you don't think that, right?"

"Ninny, what are you talking about?" I stared at her for answers.

"Your 'best friend' met me on the porch, and was being a bitch to me like I wouldn't detect her attitude, then I walk in here, and you're practically naked. So, again, you can't think I'm naïve enough to ignore the obvious."

"Again, what are you talking about?"

"This is what we are not gonna do," she said in a deafeningly low tone.

I knew what she assumed, but she was wrong. There was nothing between Kenliegh and I. Never have been and probably never would be. I wasn't in love with Ninny, but I was definitely developing feelings. She stood in a multicolored romper dress with tan buttons lined down the front and a scowl on her face.

"Jawaine, I'm not feeling it, honesty. I sincerely wanna say fuck you and this party," she spun on her heels and headed for the door.

Thankfully, mom and pop weren't home because I was hot on her trail. Grabbing her arm, I spun her around.

"What the hell, Ninny?"

"No, Jawaine. I'm not crazy, and you're not gonna tell me what I'm seeing is a figment of my imagination. Y'all are far more than best friends. I know you're fucking her."

"Nah, you trippin."

"I am, am I? Call her back over here so she can tell you how she pretty much smirked at me with an *I fucked your man* demeanor at the door."

"I don't have to call her back to tell my truth, Biansha. I didn't do anything with her."

"Well, why in the fuck were you in there smiling like a Cheshire cat? Huh? Tell me or let me the fuck go, Jawaine."

"Listen, one thing I'm not is a cheater. Either you gon' take my word for it, or you gon' walk out on me."

"Let me go then."

I threw my hands up and allowed her to make her decision. Biansha stormed down the hallway with me hot on her trail as she flopped down on my bed with a cute pouty face. It only took a year for me to see it.

"So nice to meet you, Ninny."

She glowered at me, not wanting to laugh. I was about to fix that, though. Stepping to her, I leaned my head down to take her lips in a kiss. I sucked on the bottom one sensually, causing a breathy moan to escape her. Fondling her boobs, she leaned back on the bed, and I followed suit, ending up on top of her. We kissed passionately for a few minutes, then I found myself unbuttoning her dress to find the sexy, sultriness of a smoked grey and pink lace underwear set. Eyeing her momentarily, I licked my full lips.

"Damn girl, you sexy as fuck with your lil booty having ass."

She giggled and slapped my head. Moving downward, I ended up on the floor on my knees, kissing her inner thighs before doing the same thing to her pussy through her panties. She hissed slightly as I dug my fingertips into her small love handles. Licking the length of her fat pussy lips through the material had become a challenge because her sweetness had me wanting more.

I backed up a little. "Stand up," I commanded, and she followed my orders.

Pulling her panties down, I wanted to take things up a notch. "Turn around and bend over," She did, and I held her hip, then tapped her inner thigh with my other hand. "Put this knee on the bed."

After I had gotten her into position, I kissed both of her ass cheeks and nibbled each of them following the kiss. "Damn you sexy as hell," I squeezed her cheeks. I spread her butt and licked the length until my tongue found her pulsating bud then suckled on it like a Charms Blo-pop. Releasing her pearl, I followed the split back up to her asshole and made love to it with my tongue.

Wrapping one arm around her waist to hold her in place and gently rubbing her bud with my free hand, I had her going wild. After allowing her to have an anal orgasm, I decided to flip her over and devoured her pussy the way I'd annihilated her ass. Sticking two fingers in her box tickling her g-spot, she came within seconds.

"Now, can daddy get a nut too?"

She nodded her head up and down swiftly while fingering her nipples in a circular motion.

"I don't speak sign. I said, can daddy get a nut too?"

"Yes, please fuck me, big dick daddy," she cried out.

Mind you, I don't look at other people's meatpack so I humbled myself when it came to mine. Since I had nothing to compare, I felt like my dick wasn't longer than what I considered average, but it definitely held girth. What I lost in length, I made up for in width. Plus, I had rhythm, so when I fucked my dick made music. I knew how to work a pussy like a master knew how to work a slave.

After fetching a condom from my nightstand, I dove into Ninny's pussy and punished her for the way she acted moments ago. I pulled out to the tip of my dick and catapulted the length into her. "Tell daddy you sorry for accusing him," I spoke in third person. Her pussy was so tight, it was a perfect fit for my dick.

"I'm sorry, daddy." She yelled.

"What are you sorry for?" I asked as I worked the tip of my dick at her opening before slamming it in her again.

"I'm sorry for ac–, accu–, accusing you," she stuttered.

"Are you gonna try that shit again, Ninny?"

"No, daddy, please stop playing with the pussy and fuck me hard."

"Your wish is my command."

I slammed into her repeatedly as she yelled to the top of her lungs and threw her ass back. The slapping of my nuts against her pussy had her leaking like an old drain. Looking down at her juices all over the condom and my stomach, sent me into overdrive. I thrust into her gushing wetness for several more minutes before releasing my seeds into the rubber. When I pulled out, she collapsed onto her stomach, and I followed suit.

"That was good, love," I said through labored breaths before smacking her ass.

She rolled over into the crook of my arm and kissed the corner of my mouth. "That was amazing."

After we laid there for a few more minutes, we decided to hit the shower and take a short nap before the party in two hours.

My dad allowed me to take his Mercedes Benz E-Class to the party, and I'm glad I did because the parking lot was painted with nice rides. Not to discredit my car because my shit was new. However, in comparison to the G-Wagons, Porsches, and Teslas, my Mazda 6 didn't scratch the surface of the statements being made in the parking lot tonight.

Stepping out in my Giorgio Imani casual wear, I walked around to open the passenger's door for Ninny, who matched my fly. Proudly, I protruded my arm for her to grab ahold of, before walking the distance to the entrance.

We received hand stamps for the open bar after proving we were old enough to drink by presenting our driver's licenses. Heading in, the place was lit. Daniel Caesar was on stage performing *Get You,* which was one of Biansha's favorite songs. She couldn't contain herself as she pulled me straight to the stage and slow danced with me to the live performance.

During the set break, Daniel got off stage and mingled with the crowd like a normal dude. I thought that was pretty cool. Once he made his way to me, he dapped me up and told me he was a fan and wished me well in my future endeavors.

We walked around a bit, had a few drinks, and that's when the music dropped and stopped me dead in my tracks. I couldn't believe my ears, Ella Mai! How in the hell did Unc pull that shit off?

Feelings, so deep in my feelings

No, this ain't really like me

Can't control my anxiety

Feeling, like I'm touching the ceiling

When I'm with you, I can't breathe

I lost my shit. I swear she was singing to me as I stood there mesmerized, watching the performance. It was just her and me at the moment. I forgot anyone around me had even existed, including my girlfriend. Yes, I know it was fucked up of me being that my girl stood inches away.

"Okay, baby, that's enough."

The sound of Ninny's voice broke me from the loving glare I held Ella in.

"What I do?" I smiled devilishly.

"Don't play with me." She laughed. "I'mma let you slide this time since it's Ella Mai because, I mean, she's Ella Mai but please know, I will cut you," she threatened.

I wasn't feeling the vibe when she said she'd cut me. That shit hit me hard like she'd do it for real. I wasn't too much worried because I'd never do anything to her emotionally, for her to go those lengths.

"Oh my God, she's coming babe. She's coming over. Don't look, don't look right now." Ninny said with a tight-lipped smile.

With her warning, I played it smoothly. Ella Mai stood right next to me and introduced herself to my girlfriend, while I exploded inside. I wanted to pick her up and whisk her away from the party. She was much more beautiful in person. Television did her an injustice.

After chopping it up with Biansha, she introduced herself to me, and I was starstruck like a muthafucka. "Hi, I'm... Hi..." I shook her hand. God, they were soft as a baby's bottom.

"His name is Jawaine. He's head over hills for you. I'm sorry he's retarded right now." They both laughed at my expense.

"Well, it was nice to meet you both. I'm gonna make my way around the party once you give me my hand back." She laughed.

"Baby, let the woman's hand go, please." Biansha pried Ella Mai's hand from mine.

Ella walked away, disappearing into the crowd.

"She's beautiful, right?" Biansha asked.

I was a little afraid to respond, not knowing if it was a trick question. Instead, I told her what I thought was the smartest answer. "I mean, she aight," with the both of us laughing, we made our way to the bar to re-up on our drinks.

Overall, we had a great time. I'd seen Kenleigh several times, but not once did she make her presence known. I figured she knew that she had pulled some fucked up shit with Biansha earlier. I would be sure to check her ass about it later. I wasn't about public humiliation or hot ghetto messes.

One year later…

"Uncle Bucky, how can you keep such information a secret for so many years?" I cried my eyes out once I was given the address of my mother's location.

"I didn't want anything to affect the way we raised you. The truth would have handicapped you from being the woman you are. I dare not allow anything to stand between you and womanhood. Your Aunt Junie and I worked hard to get you to where you are, Sugar Bear," he reasoned.

I understood where he was coming from, but I also didn't think anything would have changed my upbringing. So what, my mother was upstate in prison. How could that have affected me?

"Uncle Bucky, I don't understand. You and Aunt Junie were wonderful parents to me. So wonderful I probably wouldn't have known you guys weren't my parents had you not told me why I called you aunt and uncle instead of mom and dad when I was old enough to understand. You guys had custody of me since I was merely an infant."

My tears flowed continuously as he stood with empathy filled eyes. Aunt Junie took me in her arms and cried with me. I had no idea the depth of what was going on or why they would keep such information hidden and why they encouraged me to allow my mother to tell her own story.

Had she killed my father? Had she abused me so bad that I was taken out of her custody and she'd been imprisoned for it? What was it?

I needed to talk to Jawaine, but I hadn't really been in constant contact with him because I had been forbade by Jon since we'd moved in together. Although I snuck and talked to him when we moved out of state for him to play in a semi-pro football league. He'd been invited to tryout for a few pro teams during the offseason this year.

I truly hoped he'd make one of the professional teams because he's been stressed out, trying to work during the offseason and play semi-pro. I mean, of course, he made ok money, but he could work a normal job to make what he made without running the risk of concussions or broken bones. I worked to hold us down. I had a decent job, making more money than Jon, and that did nothing for his already bruised ego. His cheating had become more excessive, expected, and accepted. Nonetheless, I loved him.

"Sugar Bear, your tears seem to be deeper than what has been presented to you. What's going on, baby?" Uncle Bucky could smell a rat in the midst of a cow pasture filled with manure.

"I'm not sure what you mean. This is overwhelming, all of it. Like, am I going to find out my mother killed my father or that she's a masked murderer, a bank robber, or worse, a child molester? I'm afraid of what will be revealed."

"I'm much smarter than that, and so are you. You and I both know you're blowing smoke up my ass, Sugar Bear. You really have to wake up early to pull the wool over Uncle Bucky's eyes. Is that son of a bitch abusing you?"

"What? No. He would never hurt me."

"Maybe not physically, but don't think I'm not aware of him sleeping with the Green girl across the way. I would see him creeping out of their house many mornings. Matter of fact, is that his baby she's carrying?"

"What? She's pregnant?" I yelled.

"Bucky, stay out of this child's love life," Aunt Junie butted in.

"No Junie, this is our baby. Just like we have protected her from everything else, we should have tried harder to protect her from the good ole boy. The face of Alabama Crimson Tide football. He ain't shit!" Uncle Bucky spat. "The NFL knew it too. That's why his piece of shit ass wasn't drafted, because they recognized the *ain't shit* in him!"

"Uncle Bucky, how dare you?" I yelled.

"Sugar Bear," Aunt Junie called after me.

Ignoring her, I continued to stalk in the direction of the front door. Tears streamed down my cheeks harder and faster. My vision was clouded to the point I could barely see my next step. Hyperventilation set in just as I opened the door to exit. My head started spinning, then my world went black.

"Bucky, this is all your fault. You pushed her too far. You gave her too much too fast."

"No, Junie, I didn't. That fucking loser doesn't deserve our baby's loving heart. It's so big even she gets lost in it. She's too good for him, and he's taking advantage of her because he knows her world revolves around his good for nothing ass."

"Bucky. That's e-fucking-nough got damn it. Had I listened to my mother and father, this union wouldn't be. You and I both know the rough path it took for you to get here. You were much more of an asshole than he is."

"Maybe so, Junie. But I never had bitches smiling in your face and riding my dick behind your back. This bastard is disrespectful."

Uncle Bucky was pissed, I'd never heard him use such language.

"That may be true. But you and those bitches knew better. Y'all knew seventies Junie would've fucked y'all whole world up. I would've cut you, that bitch, and any muthafucka that got in the way. Tuh, Junie Amariah Winston was that bitch. I didn't play those hoe ass games with you and no other nigga."

"Calm down, Junie. Hell."

I wanted to laugh so bad, but instead, I stirred, pretending to be coming out of whatever I was in.

"How long have I been asleep?" I queried.

"Oh, thank the Lord. Sugar Bear, you passed out! You've been asleep for about ten minutes. Do you want water? Juice? Tylenol? Anything?" Aunt Junie fired question after question.

"No, thank you. I think I'm gonna head home to get some rest. I've been working an awful lot being that it's off season for Jon. I'm not ready to cash out on my trust fund, so I've allowed it to stay in place and continue to grow interest."

"Good idea." Uncle Bucky affirmed.

"I love you guys. I'm gonna go now."

"I'll walk you to the car, Sugar Bear." Aunt Junie informed me.

Of course, I wouldn't deny her because I knew she'd spit wisdom my way. I loved that about her. I wasn't as naïve as everyone assumed I was. I knew a bit more than I led on. I allowed people to believe what they wanted to believe about me. Aunt Junie always told me whatever someone else's problem was with me, was their problem. Fuck em.

I'd initially come over to share the news of me being engaged and pregnant, but after they gave me the package containing my mom's true identity and whereabouts, on top of revealing their hatred of my fiancé, I passed the hell out. Now I'm sitting here at a crossroad, unsure of anything, anymore. The people who raised me kept me in the dark about who I was and pretended to be happy about my relationship when they had relationship secrets of their own.

Who the hell are they?

"Give me a hug, Sugar Bear," Aunt Junie suggested.

Giving her a hug as she'd requested, I almost broke down again. I had so many questions that longed to be answered. I knew Aunt Junie could clear up the confusion that clouded my mental, but I felt she wouldn't, so I exercised restraint. She hugged me with purpose. It was like she wanted to absorb my anxiety, my pain, and my newfound need of belonging.

"Look at me," she commanded.

Looking at her with melancholic eyes, she matched my glare. I felt her spirit in my soul. It was as motherly as it had been my whole life.

"Listen to me, I know Jon was a good boy in high school and maybe even in college. So was your uncle, but he was so good he became bad and toxic for me. My parents hated to see us together, but just like you, I loved him with every fiber in my being, so I went against the grain. When my granny realized I would be with him, she warned me of the good old boys." She half-smiled.

"What did she say, Aunt Junie?"

"She said, Junie Amariah, keep an eye out on those good boys. Sometimes they turn out to be bad, and if they do, by then you're stuck because you're already drunk in love with those heart snatchers," she laughed. "She was right, by the time Bucky started acting a fool, being a lady's man, I was already in love. Mind you, his bitches knew to play their role because I would fuck their asses up."

"Aunt Junie!" I gasped.

"Oh baby, Aunt Junie didn't play the disrespectful shit. Bucky knew that shit too, so he kept his bitches at bay. Those hoes knew to stay in their lane," she advised.

"Well, how do you know he cheated?"

After looking around to see if we had any onlookers, she leaned over and whispered, "He gave me an STD, and I gave him a black eye."

We both laughed until tears spilled from our eyes. I was so glad she shared that tidbit of information with me. I didn't feel so stupid with the knowledge of how they started. Who would've known that their empire started off rocky?

"Listen to me, Sugar, not every relationship possesses what mine, and Bucky's does. We genuinely loved each other enough to get through what we went through. We prayed together, we went to church, we went to counseling, and we also spent about a year apart when you were four years old. I packed our shit up, and we left his ass alone to figure out if he wanted to be my man or everybody's man. I'd always been successful in my career as an entrepreneur. There's one thing that will scare a man that loves you back onto the right path."

"What's that?"

"When he knows that he's chosen. You have to let it be known that you want him and not need him. Otherwise, he will string you along like a puppet because he knows that you'll eat his shit and enjoy it."

"I see."

"I love you, my baby. Take care of yourself and when you find out how far along you are, make sure you call me."

"How'd you know?"

"Aunt Junie ain't a fool, baby. I didn't make it to fifty-nine being stupid. I'll let you share the news with Bucky's crazy ass cuz it ain't my story to tell. Are you okay to drive, Sugar Bear?"

"Yes, ma'am, I'm fine. I can make it home since it's only a six-minute drive. I love you so much, Aunt Junie."

Getting into my car, I buckled my seatbelt, started up, and took off in the direction of the house I shared with Jon.

Jon wasn't home when I got there. I don't know why I'd expected him to be. t was stupid of me to think so. After I'd stopped taking my birth control at his equest, I figured he wanted a baby so he could have a family. It was something he acked as a child because his mother walked out, leaving his dad to raise him and 1is brother due to his brother being born with cerebral palsy. For some time, I felt s though I could love him through the pain of her walking out of his life, now, not o much. I'm not quite ready to throw in the towels because if Aunt Junie and Jncle Bucky made it through, why can't we?

Sitting at the computer in my home office, I decided to open the box of hings that were given to me. The said contents were supposedly a collection of hings from my mother. Taking the components out one by one, they were as ollows:

-Original birth certificate

-Artifact from my father's car accident

-Letters from my mother addressed to me from several prisons along the east coast

-Pictures of me as a baby with both my parents

-The charm that donned my mother's neck in the photos in a small baggie

-Artifact from my mother's jail and prison charges

I sat up for hours reading the letters before searching the internet to find nore clues of who my mother was and why she'd been arrested and extradited to everal states. She'd been indicted for the murders of thirty-nine men along the ast coast, from Maine to Connecticut. New York had named her the "The Murderess of The Five Boroughs."

Although my father's death was ruled an accident, I wondered if my mother was responsible for his death. Had she killed him and made it look like an accident?

My original birth certificate named my mother as Trinh Tran Nguyen and my father as Kenneth Lee Peters, which I'd always knew his name. Uncle Bucky's name was Kevontae Lee Peters, and he made sure I knew about my father. The crazy part is, there were very few pictures of him around the house to say they were twins. The picture in the box proved they were definitely identical. My dad looked exactly like Uncle Bucky but with a mole under his bottom lip. Just like the one on mine.

After reading the letters from my mom, I decided to wear the necklace being that it was the first piece of jewelry that she'd gotten from my father. She never explained her charges, but she did tell me if I wanted to know, I was on her visiting list, and I could visit her.

I couldn't believe the tiny woman in the pictures was capable of murder, especially not mass murder. She was the female version of Theodore "Ted" Bundy. Out of sheer curiosity, I researched the murders. Most of them were archived, forcing me to pay to view, but I didn't care because I wanted to know. No, I needed to know.

The one thing that each man had in common was that they were married. It made me wonder, who my mother and father were? Did she also intend to kill him when they'd met? With so many unanswered questions, I had to see her. Most of all, I needed to reach out to Jawaine with all of the news.

Me: *Hey, Bestie, I sure miss you.*

Message sent 10:42 p.m.

Jay the Bae: *I miss you too. What's up, though?*

Message received 10:43 p.m.

Me: *I have a lot to tell you. We need to link up soon.*

Message sent 10:44 p.m.

Jay the Bae: *It's definitely gonna have to be soon. I'm leaving for Milwaukee to finish my master's.*

Message received 10:44 p.m.

Me: *What? Why are you leaving?*

Message sent 10:45 p.m.

Jay the Bae: *Really? You left! What's wrong with me seeing what's out there?*

Message received 10:45 p.m.

Me: *I don't want to argue. I apologize. I really need to talk to you about this package I got from Uncle Bucky today. It's on another level. Can we meet at Dauphins? I'll make the reservation. I know how much you love their Shrimp Creole.*

Message sent 10:47 p.m.

Jay the Bae: *You had me at Shrimp Creole. Text me the time, and I'm there. (smiling emoji)*

Message received 10:47 p.m.

Me: *K, love you, bestie. See you tomorrow. (Hug emoji)*

Message sent 10:47 p.m.

Surprisingly, my long-lost best friend reached out to me last night. The news she'd received had to be some crazy shit, simply because she rarely responded to my text and there she was, texting me first.

Sitting at my desk, knowing it was my last week at the precinct was bittersweet. I was a police officer when I longed to become a detective. It had been a year, and I was still street beat with what seemed to be no intent on making detective anytime soon.

"Hey, Mr. Li," an intern stuck her head around the wall of my cubicle.

"Hi, Johnna, what's up?"

"Cap wants to see you."

"Really? Why?"

"I have no idea, but he's waiting in the conference room."

"What the hell, Johnna? The conference room?"

"Listen, don't kill the messenger." She smiled and left me to my thoughts.

After throwing the last of my things into a half-empty box, I headed to the conference room.

Following the short walk, I knocked on the conference room door. When no one responded, I decided to enter at my own risk.

"Surprise!" several of my coworkers yelled. They startled me so bad I wanted to shoot all of them.

"What's this?" I grinned.

"We are proud of you, son. You beat the odds and are pursuing your education, so we decided to do a little sum-sum fa ya!"

I absolutely hated when Cap tried to be hip. He almost always failed at it. However, this time, it flowed pretty smoothly.

Looking around the room, I notice my first partner, my trainer, a few of the detectives that I aspired to be mentored by, and officers that I assumed didn't give two shits about me. There was catered food, gifts, and a few speeches. I felt special being that I was still a rookie, and they'd taken time out of their days to do this.

Cap asked me if I was okay because I hadn't eaten much of the food and he knew me, and food were best friends. I was fine, the food here would cause a problem between me and the food at my favorite restaurant. I had to meet Kenleigh later for dinner, so I'd put myself on restriction. Not wanting him to feel his effort was unappreciated, I told him I was nervous about the move. Although it was partially the truth, I honestly was a little spent about it.

When the festivities were over, I grabbed my box that was now filled to its capacity and headed to my car. Once there, my phone rang. A smile graced my face as I took notice of my baby calling.

"Hello?" I answered.

"Hi," she responded.

"How was your day, love?"

"It was great, I guess."

"What makes you guess about it?"

"Well, everything is hitting different now that it's so close to you leaving."

Closing my trunk after sitting the box in there, I hopped in my car. I took in every word Ninny had told me over the past few months, beginning with the day I applied for the program at Marquette University. True I'd finished the bachelor's program in law, but I was now interested in stepping my game up. I wanted to be a business owner, and working for the man would only provide means to get me to that point.

"Come with me, baby?" I offered.

"Come with you?"

"Yeah. We've been together for almost three years now. I don't want to give up what we've built."

"Who said we'd be giving up on us?"

"Well, no one. But the way you like to get these meat injections on the regular, you'd be deprived with me over twelve hours away."

"We were not built on sex. When I want that dick, I can catch a flight. What you thought?" we laugh at her failed attempt to mock the rapper, Young M.A. "What are you about to get into? I miss you, and I wanna get all the injections I can before you leave me."

"I'm about to head over to the seafood joint to meet up with Kenleigh. She was given a package that held clues to her past, and she wanted me to see everything."

"Really?"

"Right? I haven't heard from her in a while, so I figured she really needed to talk to someone she trusted." I responded inadvertently.

"No, I meant when were you going to tell me you were going to have dinner with Kenleigh? After you had dinner with her? Never? I mean damn, are we not a couple?"

"Bae, please don't do this. After all this time, you should know you can trust me."

"It's not about you. I don't like her, and you know why I don't."

"Ninny, are you really holding a grudge from all those years ago? Let that go for me, please. I chose you, and you chose me. It's us against the world, love."

"Okay, since you wanna say quotes like you damn Scarface or Eros, the god of love, I'mma let you have that."

"Thank you. I'm pulling up to the restaurant. I hope you plan to spend the weekend with me since it'll be my last weekend here."

"Without a doubt. We will be naked all weekend."

"Yummy. I plan to devour you each day, so I hope you ready for me to eat you up!"

"You so damn freaky."

"You like it though."

"Nah, I lov –"

"You what, now?"

"Enjoy dinner, baby. See you soon."

Ninny hung up faster than she cut her statement off. Had she finished her admission, I may have told her back. I had never cared for a woman to the capacity I care about her. My parents loved Kenleigh to no end, but they truly think Ninny is my one. My dad had even hinted at me proposing to her.

I couldn't lie and say I wasn't a different man with her. I was happier, healthier, and more content with life as it was. She was definitely worthy of the love I held inside. Being slighted by the way she skated past me asking her to come with me to Milwaukee, I didn't know if I could ask again to be let down easy.

"So, what you mean to tell me is that your mother is the female version of Ted Bundy?" I looked on in horror as I thumbed through the printouts Kenleigh handed to me in a manila folder.

"It seems so. I don't know how to feel about the whole situation. I tried to talk to Jonathan about it, but all he ever says is that if I wanted to start visiting her, he'd support me."

The sadness in Kenleigh's eyes told a different story when she spoke of Jonathan. I felt if she wanted to tell me what was going on, she would. I chose not to pry.

"Well, I for sure would take that ride with you, but unfortunately, I'll be in Milwaukee in exactly two weeks. I don't know what you plan on doing or how you want to approach the given information, but I will definitely be praying for you and the outcome you expect. Are you pissed at Uncle Bucky and Aunt Junie for keeping your mother's true identity concealed for so long?"

"In a way, I am, but I understand how it could've affected me. Imagine if I knew this information back in the day and had shared with Joneisha or something. It wouldn't have turned out well. The messy crew would've definitely used it as ammunition."

"You think so?"

"You really have to ask that question?"

"No, but I really have to ask this question?"

"What?" KeKe exasperated.

"Did you know LaShay was pregnant?"

"Was or is?"

"Same difference. Do you know LaShay is having Jonathan's child? She's due in July."

"How do you know?"

"C'mon now. She still visits her parents and approached me to let it be known one day when I was getting out of my car."

It was like a spicket started leaking as fast as the tears sprung from my best friend's eyes. Just as I'd stood to my feet to sit on her side of the table, she reached to wipe her tears, and her engagement ring near blinded me.

I can't say I didn't feel the pang in my heart since she hadn't mentioned it once. We'd been here over an hour and a half, and this is the first time that particular hand had even been visible.

"Congratulations." I expressed as I sat and held her in a friendly hug.

"For what?"

"Your apparent engagement?" I responded coolly.

"Honestly, I think he only wanted to marry me because I told him I was pregnant."

"You're what? Kenleigh, what the fuck!" I yelled louder than I intended.

"Lower your voice, Jawaine. Jesus Christ."

Looking around the crowded restaurant, I noticed several sets of oculars staring in our direction. I smiled and nodded in the burly white man's direction. He looked like he wanted to dance, but I wasn't feeling it. Taking notice of a younger couple a few tables away recording us, my blood started to boil. Everything today was based on social media and likes, there was no such thing as privacy anymore.

"How far along are you?" I said above a whisper.

"I just found out I was pregnant. My appointment is on Monday."

"You can't be considering keeping this child, Kenleigh."

"Why not?"

"You'll be tying yourself to him and LaShay for a lifetime. Are you prepared to deal with the two of them on a forever level?"

"I don't have a choice in the matter, Jawaine. I will not kill an innocent child because I wasn't careful, and I had blinders on when I chose my partner. Regardless of what people may think, Jon loves me unconditionally."

"Does he really?" I asked as I took notice of LaShay standing at the podium to be seated.

"Yeah, he does. LaShay is a thing of the past." KeKe smirked.

"I guess—" my voice trailed off.

"What?"

"Kenleigh, you ain't blind." I pointed in the direction of a very large bellied LaShay and the infamous Jon who held the small of her back while they followed the hostess to their reserved table.

"I'm over this shit."

"Are you really?"

"Just get me out of here, please."

"Let me box my food up, then we can leave."

We were seated on opposite ends of the restaurant, which left them in direct view of us but we were secluded from them. The waiter stopped back over to check on us, we paid, boxed my food and got out of there unseen. He was so into his baby mama, he didn't notice his fiancé. That was the absolute craziest shit I had ever seen. I'd heard of nonconfrontational but had I ever walked in any damn were and caught Biansha chopping it up with a nigga too comfortably, it was definitely gonna be put out there for every party to be aware of one another's presence.

Two weeks later…

Kenleigh (She)

"Leigh, where's my muthafuckin dinner at?" Jon yelled to the top of his lungs as the microwave door slammed shut.

"Sorry, baby. I cleaned the house from top to bottom and called myself taking a nap, but I slept through my alarm, which was set to wake me in time to have your dinner ready."

"Sorry? Is that all your sorry ass got? That shit ain't gonna fill me up."

"The meat is thawed. I can turn you a pork chop over and make some cheese grits in less than thirty minutes. Let me go and turn the shower on for you so the water can be adjusting." I brushed him off.

I knew he'd been partying tonight. The way his eyes glossed over told his story. He'd been drinking and doing cocaine. If he was to get drafted by the NFL, I could only see things going one of two ways. He'd either get extremely better or horrifically worse.

"I don't want to take no god damn shower. I want to eat a home-cooked fuckin' meal. You know what I think happened?"

I kept my lips sealed because I knew any answer, I'd give him, would cause him to punch another hole in the wall or drag me down the hall by my hair. He said he'd never put his hands on me but he damn sure didn't have a problem gripping a handful of my tresses and causing me to lurch behind him while looking at the carpeted floor.

"Did… You… Hear… Me… Ask… You… A… Damn… Question… Kenleigh?"

"Yes," I responded subtly to keep the tone neutral.

"Yes, what?"

"Yes, King of Kenleigh's castle and ruler of her world."

"Well, answer me, dammit."

"No, King. What do you think could've caused me to sleep all day?"

"I think you might have snuck your ass out to meet with that bitch nigga that I told you to stay away from. Do you know why I think that?"

"No, King of Kenleigh's castle and ruler of her world. Why sir, do you think that?"

"Bitch, you trying to be funny with the sir shit?"

"No, why would I want to make you mad, King?"

"Get your ass over here. You think I didn't see you with that fuck boy at the restaurant a couple weeks ago? Huh? You think I'm a fuckin fool, don't you? Is the seed in your stomach his?"

Something about his tone, his demeanor, and the glare in his eyes had me deathly afraid. I didn't want to move too suddenly or answer the wrong way.

"Bitch, do you fuckin' hear me?!" he roared so loudly my entire world shook.

"Yes, King. I heard you. No, the baby isn't his. I haven't seen or heard from Jawaine in mo –." Before I could finish my statement, Jon had dragged me down the hall and slammed me on the floor near the bed.

"Get yo ass up." He snatched me by my locks.

I'd attempted to pry his hands from my hair, but I couldn't. He lifted my nightgown up and slammed himself into me roughly. This wasn't a rare occasion, but if I was being honest, his sex was always rough. It hadn't felt like lovemaking in the history of us having sex.

"Please, Jon, this hurts. My stomach hurts."

He pulled me back by my neck, thrusting into me repetitiously, causing a shooting pain to travel from my pelvis to my abdomen. After a few more emotionless grunts, he let his seeds swim deep into my uterus then slung me to the side like the piece of trash I felt like. My legs were so weak that I fell onto the corner of the nightstand, causing me to howl in pain.

"Get your stupid ass up, take a shower, and fix my dinner," he seethed.

I attempted to get up, but I couldn't move from the spot I was in. Something didn't feel right. There was something warm oozing down my legs. I'd had semen crawl my leg before, but this felt eerily different.

"Jon, I can't move. Please have mercy on me and help me. Please?" I cried.

Blowing out a healthy breath, he stalked over to me and yanked me up by the hair. My legs felt like wet spaghetti noodles. Still, I could feel the oozing.

"What's streaming down my legs, Jon? I'm afraid to look."

"Oh my God, baby! There's gallons of blood pouring down," he exaggerated while gagging. He was freaked out by the sight of blood.

"No, there isn't. Do you hate me so much that you want to scare me? I only feel wetness on the right side."

"I need to get you to the hospital. You're bleeding pretty bad."

Of all the emotions he'd recently displayed, none of them were as caring, concerned, or kind as he was at this very moment.

"You're gonna need a pad or a diaper or something to catch all this blood, baby. What do I do? Where is your underwear? Which drawer do I go in to find some clothes? I need you to answer me!" he yelled so loud it pierced my eardrums.

Falling to the floor, I attempted to tell him where to find everything before my world went black.

"Sugar Bear, I need you to wake up to tell me your side of the story. That bitch ass muthafucka left you here to wake up to this tragedy afraid and alone."

I heard my Uncle Bucky's voice in the distance. Attempting to wake up, I tried to shake myself from the darkness that I was bonded to. I felt a heaviness on my eyelids and sadness in my soul. The pain in Uncle Bucky's voice had me shaken. A door opened and closed.

"Hey, baby," Aunt Junie said to whoever had entered.

"Hey, T Junie."

"How are you, Mrs. Junie," Biansha spoke, followed by what I assumed to be a kiss on *my* aunt's cheek because I recognized the sound.

What's she doing here? Where am I? Why can't I open my eyes?

"What happened to her?" Jawaine asked.

"We don't know," Aunt Junie said. "All we know is what the nurse was allowed to tell us about her health, which wasn't much because of HIPAA. We aren't listed on her charts, just him. Of course, he decided to call us today, right before we called Kenleigh to see if she wanted to have dinner with us tonight."

"What's HIPPA?" he fired back.

"In lament's terms, it's a violation of patient rights as far as sharing medical information." Smart ass shared. Apparently, I was in the hospital.

"They had just called for my flight to board. I'm glad I hadn't gotten on the plane yet."

"I'm gonna step out in the hallway. I can't take this. I need some air." Biansha sniffled.

"Baby, I'll be out in a moment," Jawaine voiced.

"You're still gonna leave today?" Uncle Bucky asked in shock.

"Yes sir, I rescheduled for a later flight, so I'm on the redeye. My classes will not wait for me, Unc."

"I guess I understand, son."

Uncle Bucky sounded disappointed. I needed to open my eyes. Lord, please let me open my eyes. I had to see Jawaine before he left.

Everyone had gone silent, and moments had passed. However, I had no idea how long because I was out of it and unable to keep time. I decided to pray for God to wake me up. I was now becoming really afraid.

Dear God,

I come to you as humble as I know how in prayer for strength and recovery. I'm not sure what's going on with me, but the last thing I remember was Jon coming home coked up accusing me of meeting with Jawaine. He got physical and sexual with me then from there it's a blur... God please, I need you right now.

The door opened, then I heard footsteps closing the distance.

"What's the word?" Uncle Bucky asked as whoever entered touched my body in different places.

I heard buttons pressing and paper printing. Apparently, I was in the hospital.

"No change yet. She'd lost a lot of blood when she came in and was in and out of consciousness. We are still unsure as what took place," an unfamiliar voice said.

"Oh my God," Aunt Junie gasped.

"What is it, Junie?" Uncle Bucky quizzed.

"Her baby," Jawaine whispered.

"What damn baby?" Uncle Bucky gritted.

It was then that I'd released a whimper. I felt tears streaming down either side of my face.

"Looks like she's waking up, ladies and gentlemen."

My eyes fluttered open as everyone stood around, staring at me like I was an alien. My aunt had tears in her eyes, my uncle had murder in his, and Jawaine's held sadness. With the information I'd gathered by overhearing them and the talk I had with God before fully waking up, I instantly grabbed my stomach.

"My baby," I whispered.

The solemn look the nurse gave me, told me that my worst fear had been my reality. Jon's temper was becoming a problem. I remember what happened now.

"I can't disclose any information to you in the presence of anyone without your permission. If you'd like me to bring you up to speed, I'd be happy to. Either verbally agree that it's okay to speak in their company or ask them to leave." The nurse informed me as she continued to check me out.

She flashed her penlight in both my eyes, had me push down and pull up on her hands with my hands and then my feet.

"Did I lose my baby?" I asked. That was the most important question I had, and I needed an answer.

Looking around the room at all of the awaiting sets of eyes, she peered at me.

"It's ok that they are here, please tell me."

"Yes, you lost your baby and the majority of your blood due to the internal bleeding. Thank god for technology because otherwise, we wouldn't have known what was going on. You received four units of blood as well as two sutures in your scalp where a plug of your hair was missing from."

"I don't understand." I ogled her intensely.

"Well, I was assigned to the case when you came up to the floor. ED said that—"

"ED?" Jawaine queried.

"Emergency Department, sorry. They told us that the guy who brought her in stayed until he got a phone call, saying that his girlfriend was in preterm labor on the labor and delivery floor."

"What? He left me in the emergency room to go be by her side?" I cried.

"Sugar Bear, don't do this to yourself. You knew that eventually he was gonna be there for their baby's birth, right?" Uncle Bucky asked.

"Yeah but Jesus, while I'm near death, he just leaves me."

"Well, since you are aware of the obvious, what happened? How did you get here, KeKe?" Jawaine asked.

"I fell getting out of the bed. Somehow my feet were caught in the sheet."

"And the patch of hair that was missing must got caught by the box spring?" Uncle Bucky asked facetiously.

"Bucky, that's enough," Aunt Junie scolded.

"No, Junie. That's a load of bullshit, and you know it. Everyone in here knows it. The look on her face as she explained what happened, screamed domestic violence."

"Uncle Bucky, Jon would never hit me."

"I sure wouldn't, Mr. Peters. I love that woman," Jon said as he walked in.

"Do you really?" Jawaine asked.

"Why the fuck are you even here?" Jon shot back.

"Bitch," Jawaine yelled and chin-checked Jon.

"Fuck you," Jon slapped Jawaine with the flowers he had in his hand.

Uncle Bucky grabbed Jawaine and escorted him out of the room. I don't know what got into Jawaine, but that was the second time he'd took off on Jon in my defense. He wasn't a fighter, but his dad had taught him to defend himself as he knew he'd be picked on by others on the strength that he was adopted and by Asians. Bao was the Golden Gloves champion of the lightweight division nine years in a row.

"What the fuck you got all these muthafuckas up here for? What goes on in our house, stays in our house."

"Jon, what are you talking about? I just woke up from however long I'd been out."

"Who are you calling a muthafucka you little pussy ass bitch?" Aunt Junie spoke up.

"Listen, old lady, stay out of this." Jon threw over his shoulder.

"Yeah, okay— " Aunt Junie stood to her feet to leave.

Slap! Slap! Slap! Slap! Slap!

Aunt Junie gave Jon a five-piece. I didn't see that coming, and neither did he. The element of surprise had him folded up.

"Ma'am, please leave." The nurse asked.

"Yeah, I'm leaving. And Kenleigh, if you had any sense, you'd leave too."

Jawaine (He)

"Man, I'm not gon stand by and let nobody and I mean nobody beat on her, Unc. You and Pop raised us to protect each other at all times."

"I know, son. You two have been friends for as long as y'all knew what friends meant. But is he worth your future?"

"Listen to Mr. Bucky, babe. You have your future to think about. The one thing I know about an abused woman is, it doesn't matter how many times someone else intervenes, they won't leave until they're ready."

"Yes, listen to your woman, son. Your future is standing right here. Until Sugar Bear is ready, she won't leave him. I mean, look at all the women he flaunts in her face. None of that mattered, she moved in with him, quit school, got engaged, and apparently got pregnant. What can we do for her?"

"Beat his ass!" Aunt Junie yelled. "Let's go, Bucky. I ain't with this shit. Fuck that little punk ass bastard. I'm about to lose my religion in this bitch!"

Uncle Bucky laughed so hard that Aunt Junie laughed then Biansha and I followed suit. Apparently, Aunt Junie realized she was beyond the brink of losing her religion as she lost it. Hugging them, I was preparing to head back to my parents' house so me and my girl could get it in one more time before my flight.

"Aunt Junie?" a voice called behind us.

We all turned to face the nurse who was in Kenleigh' room with questioning looks on our faces.

"I know this is out of character and I may lose my job for this, but let me get one up top." They slapped hands. "That was the best reaction I have witnessed in my twenty years as a nurse. When you lit into him, I wished I didn't work here so we could've tag teamed his ass."

"I got a job for you, honey. Let's get his ass."

"Junie," Uncle Bucky laughed.

"I'm just kidding, Bucky." She kissed his lips. "Unless you want to?" Aunt Junie looked at the nurse. They slapped fives again, and we all headed out.

We walked to the car hand in hand. I was livid about the events that had taken place, but as everyone made clear, there was nothing I could do for her. She'd made her choice years ago to deal with his cheating ways. After so long he'd become verbally and emotionally abusive.

Had I needed to take a guess, this wasn't the first time, and I'm sure it wouldn't be the last he'd gotten physical with her. I'm willing to bet my last dime on it.

"Baby, you okay?"

"Yeah, I'm good. Why, what's up?" I looked at my boo.

"You've been biting the inside of your cheek since we got in the car a couple of hours ago at the airport." She grabbed my hand. "I've noticed you do that when you're nervous, hungry, sleepy, thinking, or anything outside of your comfort zone. It's like a tick."

"You know what, you're very observant." I kissed her hand.

"I am. I've spent a lot of time with you not to know your buttons. I intend to spend a lifetime with you. Shouldn't I take an interest in your likes, dislikes, and whatever it is I needed to know to keep you happy?"

I admired the woman I'd spent the majority of my days with over the last few years and took in her unquestionable adoration of me. She ogled me with attentiveness, respect, and love. How could I not choose her to be mine forever? She'd been team Jawaine since we met. I gave up the fast lane for her, and she's held me down at every turn. I can't leave without her.

As we'd pulled into my parents' driveway, I leaned against the passenger's door and leered at her while holding her hand in mine.

"What?" she shied.

"You are so beautiful, Ninny."

"You are silly. Let's get out." She turned to open her door, but I hadn't let her hand go.

"Baby, you know I would never, right?" I referred to what had happened to Kenleigh.

"I hope not, because I will cut you," she smirked.

"Nah, I wouldn't do it and not because I'm afraid of being cut. I wouldn't do it because you don't deserve that, no woman does." I kissed her hand for the third time and released it.

My parents caught their flight twenty-five minutes after I was supposed to board. They had business in New York City. Ninny had taken us all to the airport at the same time. We decided to have the leftovers that my parents would throw out when they returned. I don't know why they stowed it in the fridge instead of the freezer.

"Wanna watch a movie?" Ninny quizzed.

"Nah, I wanna make one," I suggested.

"Ooooh, don't be such a freak."

"You like it when I'm this way," I grabbed her by the neck and tongued her down.

The breathy moan made my dick rise to the occasion. She pulled away from me and stared at my Nike basketball shorts that my manhood had made into a makeshift tent. Licking her lips, she tugged at the waistband, and I sat up, giving her leverage to free my lil dude.

Beating me off, she leaned in and licked the tip. Apparently, she had a mint in her mouth because the cool warmth of her breath felt amazing. My head fell back on the couch as she took me in whole. Filling her mouth with my manhood, I gently grabbed her hair and ground my hips as she deep throated me. Not once did she gag, which turned me the fuck on. Damn, my baby was bad ass. She wasn't a swallower, so I knew I'd be pulling out soon to give her a facial. I felt the main vein pulsating and apparently so did she, she stood to her feet, pulled her Maxi dress up and sat on my wood.

She rode my shit backward until I released every seed that I had into her guts. Holding onto her titties, she laid her head back, causing us to be cheek to cheek. Turning to her, I kissed her lips.

"Ninny?"

"Yeah," she panted.

"I love you, boo."

The stillness that filled the room after my admission had me feeling some type of way. Instead of repeating myself or asking her how she felt about what I'd said, I sat there and took in her reticence. Maybe I'd overstepped my boundaries. I decided to tap her leg so she could get up and we could shower. She sat a minute before moving. My flaccid, sticky, meat pack fell against my leg as she arose, releasing me from the suction of her vaginal walls. The sound her pussy made, had me wanting to dive directly back in.

"You wanna shower with me?" I quizzed.

"Baby, you know I wanna shower with you." She kissed my lips and left me to my thoughts while she went to draw the water for us.

Dammit, I feel so stupid. Why did I tell her I love her? It was a moment of weakness that I vow not to ever display again in life. Hell, we've been together long enough for us to be in love. Is it me? Does she not really want to be with me? Was I convenient? Was I a pastime for her while she got through medical school? In two years, she'll be a doctor. Maybe me being on the lower end of the financial spectrum, has her on edge. Maybe she thinks she'll have to carry me.

"Baby, the water is temperate. Are you coming, or am I showering by myself? I grabbed your fresh clothes."

"I'm on my way."

When I got to the bathroom, Ninny sat, spread eagle on the bathroom counter rubbing her clit. What the fuck was she up to? She just let me down easy, now she wanted more hot meat injections. What kind of games was she playing with me?

"Are you gonna stand there or are you gonna come get this pussy?"

"What do you think?"

I slid in her pussy and had to rethink the whole situation. It was hot and ready for me. I had to stand still as she squeezed her muscles around my dick.

"What the fuck you doing to me, woman?"

"Making sure you allow me time to get accepted into the fellowship before you decide to move on without me."

"What are you talking about, move on?" I asked, finally able to slide in and out of her box.

"Jawaine, I know you're a man, and you have needs," she said between cries.

"Ninny, I ain't going nowhere. You gonna have to break up with me for me to move on," I grunted as I pumped in and out of her wetness. My dick was coated with her juices, and neither of us had thought about or mentioned a condom, at all, for the past couple of days.

Damn her pussy was sucking me in like a black hole. I couldn't take it any longer.

"Baby, you been doing kegs?" I asked while working her middle.

"Doing what?" she breathed.

"Kegs? You know when you put those lil balls in your pussy to keep it tight?"

"It's kegels, silly ass man," she barely got out between breaths.

Had I not been all into this good snatch, I probably would've laughed at myself. I worked that pussy so good all she could do was lean back on the mirror to keep herself up. Leaning into her, I sucked on her neck. Not to put hickeys but to heighten the sexual bliss.

"Ooooh shiiiiiiiit!" She leaned back in and reached under my arms in a hook-like manner then threw her pussy back.

Faster and harder, I banged into her. It didn't deter her from matching my energy. The slapping of our skin against one another had us reach our peaks at the same time. I thrust into her as deep as I could and sent my seeds deep into her.

"That's probably twins," I breathed and kissed her lips.

"That's not a problem for two people who love each other," she kissed me with a passion that I hadn't felt before. "I love you so much, Jawaine. We will make a great team," she cried.

Pecking her lips simultaneously, I ground into her, bringing woody back to life. Kissing her tears away, I told her she had nothing to worry about and insured her that her heart would be my most valued possession. We made love several more times. In the shower, in the bed, in the shower again, and on my dresser as we made our way to get a second set of fresh clothes.

I couldn't believe the kid was in love. After Ninny and I finished making love everywhere, she went home to get clothes that were decent enough to sit with me at the airport. She was the best thing that happened to me since Huang and Bao, aka mom and pop.

My parents didn't cross my mind as much as they did when I was younger. I don't know if it was because I'd grown to realize things happened the way they did because it was God's will, or if it was that I'd grown to be comfortable in my skin as a man. Mind you, I still wanted to know who their murderer was, I also wanted to finish my path first. I didn't want anything hindering my growth.

Ding. Dong. Ding. Dong. Ding.

The doorbell interrupted my thoughts as I laid, staring at the ceiling. I wonder why Ninny didn't walk in; she knew I'd left the door unlocked for her. Shuffling down the hallway, I decided to look out the window before pulling the door open.

"To what do I owe this visit?" I asked Kenleigh as she stood there, distressed. Her clothes were disheveled, and her hair was unkempt.

"May I come in?"

"Yeah, come on."

Sitting opposite of each other on the couch, quietness filled the room. It was an awkward, eerie, silence, and I wasn't feeling it.

"What's up Kenleigh? I know you didn't come over to sit here, what is it?"

"I missed you."

"We had dinner last week. Why didn't you call me or text me to tell me that?"

"I couldn't," she paused.

"Why not? Don't you have a phone?"

"I do. I also have your number etched in my brain."

"SOOO?"

"Jon screens my phone calls, my text messages, my gas mileage, my length of stay, my every move. I just don't know what to do anymore."

"It's simple… leave that fuck boy."

"It's easier said than done, Jawaine. I don't expect you to understand."

"What is there to understand. He has disrespected you since senior year, and now he has caused you to lose your baby. All you ever wanted was to be a mother. What the fuck Ke?"

"I knew you would judge me; I don't know why I came here," she stood to her feet.

"Listen," I grabbed her arm. "Sit down, please. I'm not judging you; I'm simply stating the obvious. He's not gonna change. I was the obvious choice for you, but you didn't want to see what was in front of you. If you would've chosen me, you wouldn't be going through this shit. If you haven't noticed by now, the old saying is true bestie."

"What old saying?"

"Sex won't make him love you, and a baby won't make him stay."

"Aunt Junie told me that the night before I decided to give him my virginity, but I took my chances."

"And how's that working for you?"

"Every man in the world isn't like you, Jawaine. Jon made a mistake. While I love you and have loved you all our lives, I can't continue to allow you to bash him. I'm gonna go ahead and leave."

"Okay, Kenleigh, whatever floats your boat, love. If using me as a punching bag is gonna help you sleep alone tonight, while your man is with his baby and his baby's mom at the hospital, do you."

"Walk me to the door, please."

"Why? It's right there, you know your damn way."

"Listen, I know now you loved me more than I loved you. Had I realized you were in love with me all those years ago or you said something, maybe it would be us and not him. And even though he treats me like shit, had I had sense, he'd be no competition, but I don't, and that's why I'm in love with someone else."

"Okay, Kenleigh. I ain't with the riddles tonight. I have somebody so guess who isn't about to take that bullshit walk down *what if* lane with you? Me."

Standing to my feet, I prepared to walk her to the door. She grabbed my hand and kissed my palm. It was something she'd done since we were kids. It was our signature. I kissed her head, and she kissed my palm.

"I love you, best, but I'm in love with him. I'm sorry if I ever hurt you and ever strung you along, thinking we would ever be more than friends. I never looked at you beyond friendship, and that's my deepest regret." Kenleigh looked into my eyes as tears spilled down her cheeks.

Grabbing either side of her face, I pulled her to me and kissed her head. She wrapped her arms around my waist and held me there as I wrapped my arms around her neck. She looked up at me, and the sadness that filled her eyes broke my heart. The chemistry between us was unthought of, neither she nor I should've been in this predicament.

She kissed me. *Lord, I've always wondered what her lips felt like.* It was like I had a bite of heaven. Suckling on her bottom lip, I grabbed her neck and deepened the passion between us. She started to tug at the bottom of my shorts while I pulled at her shirt. Once I got her shirt over her head, I took one of her titties into my mouth as I backed her up against the door. I couldn't believe it was finally happening.

In the motion of taking her shorts down, I acknowledged the bruises all over her body, and I froze.

"No, Jawaine, why'd you stop?"

"I can't," I shook my head.

"What? You've wanted me all of our lives. You just said that," she huffed in annoyance.

"Yeah, I did. But I can't do this. You just lost a baby, you have a fiance, and I have a girlfriend. Awe man, what about my girlfriend?"

"What about her?" Kenleigh kissed her teeth.

"I love her, KeKe. I'm in love with her. I refused to do this to her. I'm not a cheater."

"You had so many women in school. What do you mean you're not a cheater?"

"Don't come for me or my girl on that type of bullshit. You know I was single when I was doing my thing. I'm in love. I think you need to go."

Grabbing her shirt after I'd found my brain and declined her of my wood, Kenleigh studied me like she wanted to kill my ass. I couldn't help but smirk at her anger. Not that it was funny, but because of the fact that I had fallen in a venus flytrap that she'd strategecially placed. I had almost been a sucker for her once again.

"I will always love you as a best friend, no one, but my wife will take that title. But as far as us ever having sex, that ain't gonna happen, I love my girl with everything in me, and she doesn't deserve being cheated on. Here you go," I handed her, her things.

She pulled her shirt over her head, tugged her pants that were half down, back up, and looked at me with adoration.

What just happened? The moment her lips touched mine. I knew everything between us would change. I stood in deep thought, the sound of her voice brought me back to the present moment.

"I respect that, Jawaine. I'm sorry about that. I shouldn't have done this."

"I accept your apology, bestie, and I wish you the best. My flight leaves in a few hours, so I'm gonna catch a few z's if you don't mind." I placed my hand on the doorknob to let her out.

"I love you, best friend."

"I love you too."

With that, Kenleigh left. The next few hours sped past, and before I knew it, I'd touched down in Milwaukee. A new life was on the radar.

Two years later…

Kenleigh (She)

Sitting in the visitation room, my palms were sweaty as my heart pounded out of my chest. It had only taken two years to build up the courage to face my mom the murderess. I couldn't believe I was here in Edna Mahan Correctional Facility for women thinking, what a way to be introduced to my mother.

I'd flown out to New Jersey for my very first face to face introduction with my mother. To say I was nervous was an understatement. Although we'd been communicating via mail and a had a talked over the phone several times, it had nothing on meeting her face to face. She'd asked me to send her pictures of me, but I'd declined to do so because I wasn't comfortable with her having them.

It didn't help that the visitation room was open, it wasn't separated by glass and a telephone receiver to speak to each other. Standing to my feet, I headed to the door to leave. I didn't care about the loss of funds spent to come here on a blank trip. Jon was now an NFL player, so we had enough disposable income to allow me to blow this joint.

Halfway to the exit, I heard a soft voice call out to me. "Kenleigh?"

Afraid to face the monster, I turned around slowly and meticulously. There stood the woman who had murdered thirty-nine men. She was so beautiful, even in her late fifties, she possessed the beauty and body of a twenty-year-old. I'm sure the expression on my face told it all.

Staring at her for a moment, she smiled. Her presence was so alluring, I understood how it had to be easy to lure an unknowing victim into her death trap.

"Were you leaving?" she asked as she took a seat at the table near where I stood.

She didn't attempt to hug me, which I was relieved because it would've been awkward. I'd never seen anyone so beautiful. I was truly blown by it; I had never been mesmerized by another woman, but she had me floored.

"Yeah, I started to think this was a bad idea. I definitely wasn't expecting to see you," I riddled.

"Did you think you'd see a big, burly, monstrous looking woman?"

"Well, honestly," I shrugged. "Yeah, I did." I chuckled. "You're beautiful."

"As you are. You look just like me with olive skin," she smiled.

We sat and held small talk for a little while and ate some of the best food I'd tasted, ever. Jawaine would've loved it here. His hungry ass would've eaten at every mini kitchen here, and there were at least ten. I smiled inwardly thinking about him and our very last encounter.

Squeezing my thighs together, I felt a gush of euphoria pass through my body.

"Hey, what was that?" Trinh's voice broke me from my reminiscent moment.

"What was what?" I replied.

"Listen, I may have been locked up for twenty-six years, but I am still a woman. Who has you smiling like that?"

"Smiling?" I scanned the room with wandering orbs. "I wasn't smiling," I bit my bottom lip.

"Okay. I guess we aren't there yet." Trinh shrugged.

"It's not that."

"What is it then?"

"It's embarrassing and unladylike."

"Really?" Trinh threw her hands up and motioned them around the room. "But this isn't?"

"You're right."

She laughed, and I fell into laughter along with her.

"I missed out on being your mom, but if given a chance, I would like to be your best friend. No secrets."

The depth of seriousness exuded in her tone of voice. It was bone chilling, which was why I trusted her from that moment forward. She would definitely slide into the best friend spot. I no longer had a best friend anyway, thanks to Jon.

"No secrets?"

"Yeah, none."

"Start with why you did what you did?" I suggested.

"Under one circumstance."

"That is?"

"You tell me why you have bruises around your neck that are poorly covered in make-up. Deal?" she stuck her hand out for me to shake.

Grabbing my neck, I'd proved to her that she'd definitely been accurate in her observation. I wouldn't back out of this conversation. History for history.

"Deal," I finally spoke, shaking her hand.

"As a girl, growing up in Vietnam, I had a rough life. Although my mother was beautiful and did everything, she needed to do to keep her home happy, my father still cheated on her. He'd chosen her, he married her, impregnated her, and still looked outside of our home for comfort sexually. Days before my fourteenth birthday, I was walking home from school, and I noticed a person in a trench coat, with the hood pulled snugly over their head, peering down an alley.

I was roughly a half block down from them when I approached, I looked in the direction at the opposite end of the footpath and and back at the person standing there. I realized the person was my mother, and she had been staring at my father having sex with a woman. I grabbed my mother's hand and yelled out to alert him of his viewing audience. Upon his recognition of us, he pushed the woman down to the ground, pulled his pants up, and ran into our direction.

My mother, Thu, held onto my hand and took off running toward our house. We had my father, Diem, beat by a quarter of a block. Upon making it across the street from our house, there was a delivery truck driving down the street, that had prevented us from crossing." Trinh paused as the tears streamed down her face.

Taking a few deep breaths, she gathered herself. During her breathing exercises, I observed a wave of relaxation as it took over her body. Her suddenly squared shoulders fell into a state of ease or obvious loosening.

"Excuse me for that. I haven't spoken to anyone about this in many years, it's painful."

"That's understandable," I responded.

"Well, anyway," she swiped a tear from her cheek, "Just as the truck got within feet of us, my mother turned to me and apologized saying she was sorry, but she couldn't do it anymore. She then lunged herself in front of the truck being killed on impact. After her funeral, my dad filed for a student visa, packed me up and moved to the United States. Not long after my twentieth birthday, he died of an overdose from too much cocaine."

I cried at the mental picture it painted for me. It was the absolute saddest thing I could imagine a child being forced to face. She handed me a napkin, and when she did, I accepted her hand into mine, offering her compassion and consolation. I couldn't fathom being in her shoes.

"The first man I killed, whom I named Scumbag Number One, had solicited me. He told me how beautiful I was and that his wife's feelings didn't matter. He said what she didn't know, wouldn't hurt her. Filled with anger and rage about how my dad may have told one of his many extracurricular whores the same crap, I lost it.

I had him rent a room in a shabby hotel, get naked, leave the money on the dresser to pay me, and I killed him. I didn't take the money; I took his life. My mentality in those days was to rid the world of dog-ass, cheating-ass men. Had I known what I know today, I would've simply lived my life happily with Kenny."

I understood her logic, but the action lacked morality and humility for humankind. It was my turn to tell Trinh something about me.

"My husband has alienated me from my best friend, Uncle Bucky, and Aunt Junie. He has not been kind to me in years. And if that's not enough, he moved Justice, his pregnant side chick into our home. She started out as a threesome for us that I was basically forced to be a part of. In our house, his motto is 'He's the king of the castle and ruler of my world.'

The bruises on my neck came from his bitch, wanting me to wake up at three a.m. to cut her some fresh fruit. Bad enough he'd defiled our marriage by inviting her in, but now he sleeps between the two of us in our oversized bed. Not only that, she fired the housekeeper, insinuating that since I didn't put in on anything, I could cook and clean the house."

Trinh eyed me as if I had lost my mind. After a few seconds had passed, she finally spoke. "While I empathize with you, the only question that comes to mind is why do you allow it?"

"I love him. I gave him everything, including my virginity, three pregnancies, and allowed him to break up any friendships or relationships I ever had."

"And how's that working for you?" she asked, bringing me back to a conversation I'd had with Jawaine.

"It isn't."

"What are the children's names?" Trinh changed the subject intending to soften the blow as she smiled.

"They were never named. Babies number one and three were forced out of me by abuse and baby number two, I lost due to stress." I sniffled.

The tears I'd been fighting to hold back had finally won the battle. They were now streaming down my face with a vengeance. The evil glare in Trinh's eyes told me that if she were free, Jon would've been her next victim and rightfully so.

"So where did the marks on your neck come from?"

"She reached over him to wake me up for fruit. I told her that her legs worked just like mine did. After I turned over and fell back to sleep, I woke up to being choked out by Jon. She stood over me with a smirk on her face and her hands on her hips. I could've killed both of them that night. Honestly, I had planned on poisoning her, but she followed me to the kitchen and watched me fix her snack."

"Bitch would be dead in my house."

"You don't say," I looked at her with a smile on my face.

"I'm in the hot seat, what do you want to know next?" Trinh asked.

"My dad, did you kill him, or had you planned to when you met him?"

"No and no. He owned a bookstore in Brooklyn. I'd been looking all over town for a certain title, and he was the only one who had the original print. I'd traveled from New Jersey, and when I got there, he had the most beautiful smile, and his aura was perfect. He wouldn't give me a chance that day, but I noticed he didn't have a wedding band, so I decided to go to his store every day to purchase a book until he noticed me. From there, it was history, we dated two years, got married, and a few years later we had you."

"What happened to him?"

"He died in a car accident, running away from me."

"You said you didn't try to kill him, so why was he running away from you?"

"There was a fortieth victim. I had gotten sloppy, so I left before I was sure he was dead. Once he recovered, he described me to the police and flyers were plastered everywhere. He came home to confront me with one of the sketches, and although I didn't confess, the continuous tears and my deafening silence admitted my guilt.

He asked me to turn myself in, but I tried to convince him to leave the country with me instead, so we could start fresh. Instead of packing up like he said he would, I walked to the room and he was on the phone with Bucky. Bucky apparently told him to call the cops, so he attempted to, and that's when I came in and disconnected the phone line. He told me he was gonna turn me in since I wouldn't turn myself in. With tears in his eyes, he kissed me passionately, kissed your forehead, and peeled out on two wheels headed to the police station.

I had packed a few of our things and was headed west about forty-five minutes later. There was traffic lined along the street as we'd run into a roadblock. As the police directed us around a car that had went head-on with a light post, I recognized it to be Kenny's. Throwing my car in park and jumping out, I ran to the taped-off area screaming he was my husband. Once I was down at the precinct for questioning, I turned myself in. My hatred for my father and any man like him, had been the reason behind the death of the only man that ever loved me."

"So, you aren't a heartless killer like the New York Post said you were?" I said, trying to break the ice. The sadness in her eyes stung like a mad bee.

"Oh no, I am," she laughed. "But he was my peace, my solace, and my sunshine during the dark hours. Although he had no idea who I was, I didn't change the fact that I loved that man with my whole heart."

We both laughed, it was a refreshing moment. Not only did I gain a new friend, but I was able to talk about what was going on with me without being judged. We agreed to see one another every month and to talk once a week.

Walking into my home, I had a new lease on life. I looked around at all of the expensive things that held absolutely no significance and felt worthless. Was this what I'd sold my soul for? My parents had more money than I could count. The value of what my dad left me, would swallow Jon's net worth and burp it out, because it wouldn't be enough to digest.

In my mind, I was free. I was tired of hearing him rant and rave about being the king of his castle and telling me that my job as a wife was to treat him as a king because he made the money, so he made the rules. I was over it; I was getting the fuck out of here. No more was I going to allow his arrogance to take me down. Our communication was nonexistent. He was controlling, jealous, and abusive... No more!

As I picked up the empty packages scattered around the movie room, I decided to do something about me feeling belittled by the people I shared my home with. Walking into the master's bedroom, I took in the sight of my husband fucking the dog shit out of his pregnant mistress. I watched for a few minutes as his less than average-sized dick, pummeled in and out of her creamy pussy and she moaned in ecstasy.

Justice finally opened her eyes and noticed me standing there. The smirk on her face boiled my blood. After picking up on my vibe, she allowed her eyes to roll in the back of her head. She threw her hips in a circle, and I lost my damn mind. I grabbed the umbrella from the hanger and started to beat the shit out of Jon. Hitting him everywhere possible, he rolled over in horror.

"What the fuck!" Jon yelled.

"This bitch has to go neeeeooooow!" I responded.

I breathed fire while I jumped on him, punching him in the face with closed fists. He was so stunned that he froze up like a bitch while I held onto his mohawk and banged his head into the headboard. He finally decided to grab my arms, causing me to knee him in the nuts. Rolling out of bed, standing on my feet, I further whooped his ass.

The more I thought about the shit I'd put up with, the more outraged I'd become. I was huffing and puffing as one of the bitches who aided him in ruining my life, looked on in horror with only her eyes peeking from underneath the sheet.

"Why the fuck are you still here you two dollar whore? Go on now, get!"

"She's not going anywhere. I run my shit, you just live here. Now shut the fuck up."

"Oh… okay," I nodded my head, pursed my lips, and started swinging on him again.

Grabbing the nearest thing to me, I went wild. Before I stopped to take in the sight before me, I heard Jon scream out in agony.

"My arm," he yelled. "My arm is my money. I'mma kill you if you fucked my arm up, bitch!"

"Oh baby, let me see," Justice cried.

"Bitch, I dare you to touch him." I breathed fire. I grabbed her by her cheap weave and slapped lightening from her face. Once the first one connected, I lost count. However, I felt liberated. "Get your fucking shit and get the fuck out of my god damn house before I knock that baby out of your stomach, ho'."

With red marks on her caramel skin, she eyed him for answers, further pissing me off. "Get to moving you homewrecking cum bucket." I whacked her across her legs with he umbrella for good measure.

"How dare you hit a pregnant woman?" she whined.

"I'll fuck you up if you don't get out of here. This is my muthafuckin' house, and you will get your plastic grocery bag of shit that you came with and get out."

"Justice, please leave," my husband begged.

"Where the fuck I'mma go Jon. You said you were divorcing her for me. You said she couldn't keep her babies and you was tired of her infertile ass," she threw out as his eyes bucked from his head.

"Is that what you said? Is that right? Are you filling your whores' heads with sob stories, you selfish son of a bitch! You knocked my first baby out of me by slamming me into a nightstand in a cocaine-fueled rage. You took your first pregnant bitch out to eat and took notice of me and my best friend having dinner. Your ego was crushed because of your own insecurities, and you took it out on me."

"First baby mama?" Justice questioned in a low voice.

"Oh, you didn't know. Did you think you were the first one?"

"Shut your mouth," Jon gritted.

"You stressed the second baby out of me by sleeping around with diseased-ridden whores. Bitches all at the health unit trying to fight me, then the same bitch come to find out, was three months pregnant, right along with me."

The tears that filled Justice's eyes should've made me feel better about the situation, but I'd already beat her down in a slap fest. Hearing the bullshit, he'd fed her, I felt sorry for her. She was another me, she believed everything his lying ass said. I honestly wanted to go to her and hug her.

"Hmh? Let's see… baby number three," I paused to contain my tears and my anger.

Looking around the room, I grabbed one of my Jimmy Choo boots and crashed it into the mirror on the curved dresser that was custom made to my liking, on my dime.

"You pushed me so fucking hard into this dresser when I contested your suggestion to allow this bitch to defile our bed in a threesome," I paused. "I hit my head on the original mirror, adopted this scar, and fell on my stomach," I pulled my hair back to show my year-old scar. "The impact was so hard that my placenta detached from my uterine wall, causing me to miscarry a third time.

Tell her again how I can't carry a baby to term. Lie to her again about how you didn't get two of your whores pregnant before her. Junior is almost four, and Savannah is two and a half.

"Junior?" Justice cried. "How in the hell are you planning to name our son Jon Junior if you already have one?"

"Listen, get your ass up, and get out my fuckin' house before I break your nose. Y'all's asses can have this discussion on your own time because I know this isn't the end of your relationship."

"I'm so sorry. I had no idea that things were this bad between you two," Justice admitted while gathering her things.

"Before you go, grab him a bucket of ice so he can take care of his children. Luckily it ain't his throwing arm, so he'll be fine."

"I hate you, Jon. Yes, hate's a strong word, but you deserve whatever this woman gives you. We are done, don't contact me about anything but our son. You know the due date, so I'll reach out with delivery dates. I don't give a damn where I go, as long as it's away from you." Justice walked out of our home without getting the ice. Maybe she was done. Perhaps I was the only one idiodic enough to ride along with his bullshit.

"Here, you stupid bastard." I slammed the bucket into his stomach, causing him to grunt.

"What's up with you? Where's this new attitude coming from? Let me find out you fucking somebody, and I'll rock your world."

"You ain't gone rock a damn thing over here. There's a new sheriff in town, and I'm no longer taking your shit."

"How was your visit with your mother last week?"

"That was today, jackass. It's none of your god damned business. If you cared, you would've come with me. The key to a successful marriage is one-hundred percent communication. We've lacked that since we started dating. I'm no longer your arm candy, find another bitch to flaunt on your arm to these events."

"I'll divorce you before you embarrass me like that with the media hounds."

"I'll bet any amount of money you won't," I shot back.

"Try me. Two words, prenuptial agreement. Remember one thing, you assumed I was too naïve to try and take you for everything you have, so you didn't make me sign one."

I smirked as he sat in a daze looking crazy as hell. Topping it off with the icing on the cake, I had to have one last word.

"Spousal support and half of your shit will do me well. Oh, and along with what my father left in trust for me, shit, I'm larger than Hajia Bola Shagaya.

"Who the fuck is that?"

"She's a Nigerian self-made multimillionaire, moron."

"Dr. Franklin-Li you have a visitor," Ninny's receptionist called into her office. I liked the fact that she was on her job, but damn, I need her to get with the program and know that when I step foot in this place, I'm Mr. Franklin-Li.

Sitting in the comfy chair in the waiting area, I thought about how life had been since the move. It had been exhilarating, I was abundantly blessed with a baby on the way, and I was also a newlywed. I'd invited everyone I remembered from back home as we decided to have our wedding here in Milwaukee, being that this was home for us now. Ninny had her private practice, I made detective last year, and I owned a catering company.

"Hi husband," Ninny said as she approached me. I stood to my feet a pecked her lips.

"I'm sorry sir, I didn't know you were Doc's husband," the obviously new receptionist shied.

"No problem, love. Take a mental note for next time." I winked.

"Are you flirting with my staff?" Ninny laughed.

"Hell nawl, you see this beautiful, sexy, pregnant woman in front of me?" I smiled as I rubbed her belly that held our six-month-old fetus.

"What's up, baby?"

"Nothing just came by to see what you wanted for dinner and to see if you had time to grab lunch."

"I do have time for lunch and dinner is in your court. As long as I get apple pie and vanilla ice cream, I don't care what the main course is.

"Let's go to the Harbor House."

"Why did I know you'd pick that place? I don't have time for that right now. I have an appointment in an hour, so we're gonna have to do a burger or something."

"Okay, I guess," I said, giving her the puppy dog eyes. Unfortunately, it didn't work.

Leaving her office, we rode in her car to The Anchorage to grab a couple of burgers since it was literally an eight-minute drive from her location. We parked and walked into the establishment. With her belly being so big because she was pregnant, we decided on an open table to accommodate her comfortability.

We ate and talked, and it was refreshing. Every moment with my wife was like we were dating for the first time. I was blessed to have had such a great relationship with such an amazing woman.

Heading back, I decided to stop off at a flower shop. Although she contested my decision, I had to get her a bouquet of yellow roses so she could know the depth of my appreciation of her. The woman who had stolen my heart, had also taken my last name and was carrying my seed, mine. Who knew this was in store for us? I couldn't be a happier person.

After pulling up to her office, I got out to open her door, kissed her lips with intensity, and handed her, her car keys and the bouquet. The moment between us was like one from a storybook. The sun was shining, the birds were chirping, and if I didn't know any better, I might have seen Jesus peeking through the clouds with his thumb up.

I stopped by the grocery store to pick up the things I needed dinner and headed home. We lived a couple of miles from the grocery store, so it only took a few minutes to get there. Once I arrived, I washed up, prepped what I need to for dinner, then took a hot shower.

An alert came across my phone, notifying me of an email. It was my personal email, which I rarely used these days. I'd reached out to several people about writing a book that I had an idea for. Most of the publisher I reached out to only deal with the fiction genre but the last person I reached out to, lead me in the right direction. I was hopeful that the email was pertaining to that.

Taking notice of the time, I ran around frantically preparing dinner, checking the email had become a misplaced memory. I placed the apples, and the fixing for the apple pie in the homemade crust, then put it in the oven blanched the asparagus, and pan seared the salmon since the wife had denied me of my seafood craving for our lunch date earlier.

After everything was done, I decided to take the ice cream from the freezer because Ninny liked hers the consistency of soft serve. I wasn't a fan of it that way, but for her, I'd walk across quicksand.

Opening the freezer, my worst nightmare had become a forefront reality, no damn ice cream. I can't tell my pregnant wife I prepared this great meal without ice cream. She'd kill me had she made it all the way home, and there wasn't any. Picking up the phone, I decided to make the dreaded phone call asking her to stop by the grocery store for it. I prepared myself to be scolded about it.

"Hey, baby," she sang in a great mood.

"Hey, can you stop to get ice cream? I thought we had some, but apparently, the ice cream bandit stopped through and ate it all." We laughed.

"Yeah, this baby of yours loves vanilla bean just like it's mommy. If you wanna keep us calm, feed us ice cream."

"Hopefully you hadn't passed the store up yet."

"Nope, I'm actually at the intersection of it waiting for the light to change, you're in luck."

"I'm in luck?" I queried.

"Yes, you. Had we not had ice cream to accompany my homemade apple pie, it would've been the rumble in the Bronx." We laughed.

"You're shaking your fist, aren't you?"

"Is…" she kissed her teeth.

"Okay, the parking lot is packed, so I'll just go to the corner store for the five-hundred-dollar ice cream."

"Five-hundred-dollar ice cream?" I questioned.

"Yeah, you know how inconveniently priced convenient store merchandise is."

I shook my head at her. She was a doctor, I had my own lucrative business and worked as a well-paid detective, but she was still frugal. That was my baby, though, with her cheap ass.

"Oh," I laughed, finally tuning back in.

"I left my flowers in the office to brighten up the place. All of the M.A.s loved them. They think you are so sweet. Then the poor new girl Jamie, she was so apologetic for not allowing you entry to my office."

"It's cool. I will only give her shit about it for a little while."

"Ok, I'll put you on video call right now so I can go into the store."

"Nah, call me when you get out."

"No, I want you to watch me do what you should've done when you went to the grocery store."

"Man, whatever. That's why I'mma tear your ass a new one when we finish dinner."

"As long as you hit that one spot like you did last night, you can tear me a few new ones."

Switching the voice call to a video call, her beautiful face filled the screen. I bit my bottom lip in anticipation.

"Stop being nasty."

"What?"

"I know you thinking about some nasty shit the way you biting your lip."

"Let me see them titties baby."

"What? No!" she giggled.

"Why not, baby? If you asked to see my dick, I'd let you. Even with it being soft and ugly like a Vienna sausage in a turtleneck sweater."

"Oooouch. Be careful in there, little one." She smiled. I noticed her shoulder moving.

"Are you rubbing your belly? Hurry up, so I can do all that for you. And the reason he's kicking you is that he wants you to show me them titties, lil booty," I grinned.

"Shut up! Who said it was a he?" Ninny's face turned up into a scowl.

"Whoa, slow down, killer. I'm just saying, yo' ass been looking nice and I heard boys do that to you."

"Boy, you so damn silly." She paused, "Hi, how's it going tonight?" she spoke to someone in the background, but I couldn't quite make out what their response was. "I don't know why they always have that lil girl working in here by herself. I couldn't do it, it's too many crazy mofos out here."

"I'd be less of a man because I'd be sitting at your job every damn day."

"Which one baby?" she asked, holding up a carton of Blue Belle's and then an off brand I'd never heard of.

"Seriously? Bring that cheap ass shit home, and I'm not leaving to pick up the good kind."

"You're right." She smiled, looking down at the obvious choice. "Well, it's final, I'm about to go che–"

"Open the fuckin register, bitch, and if you make any sudden moves, I'mma blow your muthafuckin' head off!" I heard a man say in the background.

The look on Ninny's face was that of a child who was afraid of their mom.

"Baby what the fuck is going on?" I quizzed or clarity as I put my shoes on and grabbed my keys.

She was walking pretty fast as I saw the colorful merchandise behind her like a speeding car on the highway. She put her fingers up to her mouth, asking me to be quiet as tears streamed down her face, and she slid down behind something I couldn't make out.

"I'm on my way, baby," I yelled as she looked from left to right.

"Baby, be quiet. Please, before they hear you."

"If anyone is in this muthafuckin store, bring ya asses out!" the voice commanded.

"Baby, it's a little girl crawling toward me what should I do?"

"Turn the camera to her so I can screenshot her face."

Ninny turned the camera, and I took a screenshot of the girl who was in route to her. The girl seemingly had tears in her eyes and rightfully so. If I were her, I'd be wailing. I was already in route to the store. Using common sense, I decided to keep quiet being that we were on a video call.

My mind raced a million miles per minute, I needed to alert the cops, but I also needed to stay on the line. Since I'd let my personal cell go and only used the department provided one, I was screwed. I made a mental note to add a line to Ninny's account, after dinner.

"Are you okay?" Ninny whispered to the little girl.

"Yeah, I'm okay." She responded.

"It's okay, my husband is on the way. We're gonna be fine."

"Daddy, someone is back here. She saw my face and said her husband is on the way. You need to hurry up so we can get out of here!" The girl yelled. She definitely didn't sound like the youthful, frightened kid I saw in the video.

I heard footsteps in the background, then the alarm sounded off. The footsteps that were approaching faded away, then I heard someone scream before a gunshot rang out.

"I love you, baby. If I never told you how much, please, know I love you more than life," Ninny cried.

The footsteps came back. "One hundred and thirty-six funky ass dollars. This bitch hit the alarm on us for that shit. Now, if you wanna leave alive," whoever the man was paused and snatched Ninny by her hair, causing her phone to fall to the floor face down. "You better have more than a hundred-thirty-six-dollars bitch!" he gritted.

"I'm sorry, I don't carry cash. I swear if you take me to the ATM, I'll get you five thousand. Please, I'm pregnant."

"Bitch, I'm a fuckin' junkie. Do you it look like I give a damn about you being pregnant. I see your muthafuckin' stomach, I didn't think it was a tumor. Let's walk to the ATM at the front of the store. The fuck you think, I'm stupid no'?" I heard their footsteps walk away.

The distance to the store felt like a road trip to Miami. I couldn't get there fast enough. Just as I'd approached the intersection, I espied the police lights in the distance. The girl picked up the phone and walked to the front of the store.

"Say goodbye to your beautiful wife. Hope the next one you choose will be as pretty as her." The girl from earlier smiled evilly, as I took another screenshot of her face.

Turning the camera to Ninny, it allowed me to take in her beauty which was filled with fright and her face wet with tears. She tried her best to be brave. "God, I come to you asking you to forgive me of my sins and to accept both my and my unborn child's souls into the gates of Heaven." She chanted a prayer to the Lord and my heart ached with fear and filled with hatred for the robbers.

"Ninny, no. Dammit, you are not gonna die. I see the police and the store."

"Oh, she's gonna die," the guy said. "Let him see, Baby," he called to the girl.

The girl turned the camera to the guy who turned the gun to Ninny's head and pulled the trigger. He then dumped the remainder of the bullets into her body. Not even ten seconds later, I whipped into the parking lot alongside the police. It so happened to be a couple of the officers I'd worked closely with down at the precinct. One of them held me in my car while the others secured the perimeter and attempted to enter.

"Let me out, Jones," I demanded.

"Li, you know better. I can't let you out during a–."

Just as Jones attempted to talk me down, he fell to his knees to take cover as more gunshots rang out.

"Let me out Bo, I need to help y'all. They already killed my wife."

Officer Bo Jones looked at me with sadness, then backed away from the car door. He'd been in our company several times, both socially and personally. Him and his wife were chosen to be our child's godparents. I crouched down until I got to the trunk of my car and suited up. We joined the fellas near the entrance, I went around to a window located on the side of the building and peeked in. The only thing I could see was the girl behind the counter, and it looked like she was still breathing.

I whispered to Bo that one of them was alive. I didn't want the maniac lunatic to finish her off. He called out to our fellow officers that we needed to move in order to save the one victim. I knew that Ninny had been shot several times, but I held out hope that she was also still alive.

We approached the front entrance, and gunfire rang out, blowing the glass above us and between us out of the windows and doors. The idiot had given us easier access to him and his accomplice. With all of us having a clear view of the perps, we got ready to make our way inside. One of the guys had already called for backup, so our reinforcements were on the way.

Peeking into the small hole, I saw the perps standing side-by-side talking. Apparently, they were trying to devise a plan to escape but they were surrounded, making getting away for them impossible.

"Come out with your hands up!" Officer Ojun yelled.

"Fuck you!" the male voice responded.

"Listen, if you wanna live, bring your asses out with your hands up," Bo said with force.

"Hands up, don't shoot!" The girl sang out.

It pissed me the fuck off how she had the audacity to make a mockery of our brothers being killed by the oppressors. But here she and her dope fiend boyfriend, husband, or daddy are out here killing our own kind to feed their drug addiction.

After signaling the guys, I sent a shot in through the window piercing the girl's shoulder. She yelped in agony, which, in turn, transformed her boyfriend into a raging bull. He pulled the trigger on his gun simultaneously until he had no more bullets left.

"I'm sending my fiancé out. Please don't hurt her, she's only seventeen, and she's pregnant," he begged.

The fucking nerve. This muthafucka had just killed my pregnant wife, and now he wants us to spare his cokey dokey head ass fiancé? They must've been smoking on some cheap shit. Still peering through the window, I looked on as he kissed his girlfriend and took cover inside of the walk-in cooler. I knew he was out of bullets, but what I didn't know was if he had another clip.

Throwing her hands in the air, she shuffled her feet toward the door. "I'm coming out," she yelled.

She kept her hands held in the air as she approached the door. Ojun motioned to put his gun in the holster, then she came out of nowhere with a piece of glass, cut the arm Ojun reached for her with, and lunged forward attempting to stab him. Fortunately for him, he still had his piece in hand as he pulled the trigger mere seconds before she was able to be successful. He dumped two into her gut, sending her stumbling back as she dropped her weapon to the ground. Grabbing her stomach, she took sight of the blood and let out a curdling scream. I watched as the girl reacted to what happened and felt no remorse for her. Her breathing became labored as she fell to her knees then dramatically onto her side.

Pushing past her body that was sprawled on the ground, I wanted to kick her in the face, but I wouldn't do that to a woman. Instead, I ran to my wife, who laid there as beautiful as the day I'd met her. With the exception of the bullet hole in her head, she looked peaceful.

"I'm sorry I didn't tell you I loved you back, Ninny. I'm sorry I couldn't save you. I was supposed to be your superman, the one who protected you from all evil. I love you forever," I kissed her bloody lips.

Unwilled tears sprang from my eyes. At that moment, I was as weak as a foal at birth. The woman who taught me how to love myself enough to truly love someone else, laid in my arms, lifeless.

"Come out with your fuckin' hands where I can see them," Bo yelled.

The freezer door opened and out walked the muthafucka' responsible for the travesty. He looked at me with anguish in his eyes, like he gave a fuck what I was going through. Kissing my wife's lips for the last time before they turned cold and rigor mortis started to set in, I held her in my arms. As they approached me, I picked my gun up from the floor and unloaded my clip into his chest. That no good bastard didn't deserve to breathe the same air as I did.

Family, friends, and coworkers alike filed into the church followed by the burial grounds back home for Ninny's funeral. It was the hardest day of my life being that they had to remove the baby from her, thus leaving me to bury my wife and child in separate caskets. There wasn't a dry eye in the place, being that it was a double funeral.

I lost my mind when they lowered the two caskets into the ground right next to each other.

Surprisingly, Kenleigh didn't show up to the funeral. There was no way in hell that I would've missed something so detrimental in her life. I don't care who didn't like it, they would've had to learn to deal with it. It wasn't like she didn't know. Uncle Bucky had called, emailed, and sent her a text message.

I'd stayed in back home in Alabama with my parents until I decided to stop feeling sorry for myself. The depressed stated I'd allowed myself to sink into, had gotten to a point that I had to take a leave of absence from work. I'd definitely be learning to greive one day at a time. After almost six weeks, I was contacted by the Human Resources department to ask if I wanted to resign and return when I felt it more appropriate. I thought it was insensitive of them, but at the same time as a business owner, I understood that work still had to be done.

The couple that murdered my family and my future was wanted in several cities throughout Wisconsin. They were named the new age Natural Born Killers. They weren't shit but a couple of dope addict losers in my eyes. The girl Jeanette Jamison had barely turned seventeen. She was considered a runaway back when she was fifteen. The guy, Jimmy Croutington, was a thirty-one-year-old, ex-pimp and child trafficker. The world was better off without them.

Five years later…

"Kenleigh, I'm not playing games with you today. Get your ass in there and put the fuckin' gown on that I bought you to match my tux. It's the Finnerty's Player's Ball, and I'm not going by myself." Jon yelled in my direction as I sat at the vanity.

Finnerty played free safety on the same football team as Jon. I had no interest in going to the Pimp's and Ho's themed party. If only Jon knew that Finnerty wanted me, he'd fall out and die. Finnerty had approached me at another teammate's party telling me that he'd love me like I was supposed to be loved. Little did he know; I wasn't into bouncing from friend to friend. Granted, he was sexy as all get out, it wasn't my cup of tea to be a homie hopper. However, I simply wasn't that type of woman.

"Listen, Jon, I don't give two shits about that party or the jazzy talk you spitting. You not about to touch me and I'm not gonna move any faster." I'd had enough of his verbal abuse.

Thirteen years with this man and I was over him. I had given my everything, and he didn't appreciate any of it. After I'd beat his ass a few years ago, the physical abuse had stopped. He'd found out on that day, five years ago that I'd fight his ass back. I guess that had put a little fear in his heart.

We were knocking on thirty now, and it was close to the time for his retirement from football. With all of the child support that comes out of his salary, he couldn't afford to keep the lifestyle he was living, he needed me more than I needed him. I'd started a business four years ago after finally finishing my degree. It was a processing firm like Uncle Bucky's that also specialized in private investigation. My agents and I were something like Joey Greco, we caught people cheating.

"Look, I'm asking you not to mess this up for me. I need this. No, we need this."

"Jon, nothing about us is *we*. You need this, let's not get this shit misconstrued."

"Leigh, how many years is it gonna take for me to apologize?"

"None. I don't need any more apologies; I need to live my life. When I gave you my all, you gave me your ass to kiss. Now, I'm giving you mine," I said as I pulled the divorce papers from my vanity drawer and handed them to him.

"What the fuck is this?"

"I'm sure you can read. Now that all your baby mamas are after your coins, not letting you fuck when you want to, you want me to go up to bat for you. Now that you ain't the big shot dick slinger you use to be you finally want to be in a relationship with your fucking wife. I'm good, love." I giggled.

Thinking of my last encounter with Jawaine, whom I haven't seen in many years, I smiled.

"I can't," he shook his head.

"What? You've wanted me all of our lives. You just said that" I replied feverishly.

"Yeah, I did. But I can't do this. You just lost a baby, you have a fiance, and I have a girlfriend. Awe man, what about my girlfriend?" He said, frantically grabbing his head.

"What about her?" I kissed my teeth.

"I love her KeKe, I'm in love with her. I refuse to do this to her. I'm not a cheater," he admitted sternly.

The kiss we shared changed everything between us. I would never see him as the scrawny neighbor/best friend that I use to. That's for certain, whew chillay! Just thinking about it, I almost had to fan myself.

His wife died some years ago, and I was forbidden attendance of the funeral. In order to keep peace inside my home with my husband, I'd agreed. If Jawaine is anything like he was back in the day, I'm sure he's still pissed that I didn't show up for him.

"Kenleigh," Jon growled in my ear as he pulled my head back by my hair.

"Let my got damn hair go," I gritted through closed teeth. "What the fuck is wrong with you, nigga?"

"I've been letting you slide for too long. Your ass done got outta pocket, so I see I'm gonna have to put my foot down," he fussed.

I smiled like a maniac. He'd lit a fire inside of me. I had been visiting my mom in prison monthly, speaking to her on the phone three times a week, and definitely taking her advice on how not to take his abuse. I had also taken her advice on something else she'd mention should this situation resurface.

Pulling my chrome and pearl .380 from its hidden compartment under the vanity, I shoved it into his groin as I was still in a seated position. "I've allowed you to control the best years of my life with every form of abuse there was. I'm done with the bullshit, Jonathan. Now let... my... mutha... fuckin... hair... go!" I enunciated every syllable in every word. Who was not about to start back playing hand games with him, was me?

"Now, I'm gonna go to the party with you, and if I so much as feel any form of disrespect from you and any of your little whores, I'm gonna nut the fuck up. Understood?" He was silent. It was like he needed a moment to comprehend what I'd said to him, and I didn't like that too much. "Muthafucka, I said, do you understand me?" I asked again.

"Yeah, I hear you. Can you get your gun off my dick?" He stared at me with hatred and animosity in his eyes.

"Since this is our last party together, we may as well enjoy it," I suggested.

"What you mean last party, Kenleigh?"

"It's self-explanatory jack-ass."

"You just gave me the papers today. Are you not gonna allow me time to win you back?"

"Why would I do that, Jon? You had thirteen years to do right by me. Instead, you got three kids, and I have none. You have peace, and I have drama. You sleep well at night, and I got to worry about my car being vandalized. You are flocked to everywhere you go, whereas I worry about being pepper sprayed by one of your bitches walking out of a public place," I giggled at the freedom that coursed through me. It was like a multiple orgasm that I'd read about in one of author Mesha Mesh or Pamesh's Urban novels.

"I love you, Leigh. I want us to work," he cried, literal tears.

"Do you? Really?"

"C'mon, Leigh. You know damn well I love you."

"Nah, you never loved me. I'm sad that it took me so long to come to that painful but obvious realization. The movers will be here Saturday for my things, after tonight's event, I'm moving into a condo until the divorce is finalized. You didn't accept my love when I gave it freely, so allowing you to work for my heart won't happen after years of being used, abused, and made to feel unworthy."

Jonathan stood looking lost for a few minutes before sliding over to the closet and putting his shoes on. I was hoping I didn't have to put a bullet or five in his torso because I was ready.

After finishing up my make-up, I decided to post a pic on Instagram with #CrayonCase #SupaCent #BeatFace #WazzamSupa. She had the best palates in the color wheel, and I'm glad I decided to invest in the backpack. I applied my butterfly lashes that were purchased from Nikki's Sweet Lashes, LLC, slid my feet into a pair of coffee brown Jimmy Choo's, and grabbed the matching clutch before heading to the foyer to wait on my soon to be ex-husband.

"You look beautiful," Jon leaned in to kiss my cheek. Of course, I curved him. I wasn't going to allow him to think he could woo me into not divorcing his ass. There wasn't a snowball's chance in hell of that happening.

"Look, are you ready to go before I change my mind?" I rolled my eyes.

"Yeah." He grabbed his keys from the keyholder, and we headed out.

Pulling up to my new condo, I took in my surroundings and released a breath that I didn't know I was holding. The air around me smelled like freedom, and I was basking in its ambiance.

Getting out of my car, I walked up to the door and paused, taking in my newfound independence. For the first time in my life, I would be living on my own. I was both excited and afraid. Luckily for me, my firm set up surveillance for my safety and peace of mind.

I'd stopped off at the grocery store after loading my last luggage into my Mercedes Benz McLaren to pick up groceries for dinner. I figured since it was my first night alone in my new place, I'd make a dinner fit for a queen. Being that Jon didn't like seafood, I wasn't allowed to cook it in *his* home, I went big. Lobster tail, steamed mussels, garden salad, and Jawaine's famous apple pie.

Jawaine was definitely on my mind a lot lately. I wished I could reach out to him, but I was afraid of rejection and rightful anger or disappointment for my hiatus. We'd been best friends and inseparable from the moment he moved into the Li's home. My Aunt Junie and his mom were best friends and something like business partners. Huang was the plug with the hair and products Aunt Junie needed to start her hair store, the rest is history.

The essence of dinner violently attacked my nostrils, causing my stomach to growl and my taste buds to feel violated. I hopped into the shower, threw on a t-shirt and panties, then sat down in preparation to eat. After eating I tuned into the new series that was recorded on DVR called *The Games People Play*. Although I thought it was a pretty decent show, I found myself dozing off.

Not soon after getting into bed, I drifted off to sleep and found myself dreaming of Udias. He was the character in *True Love Never Dies* by a new author named Prodigal Son. For it to be his first novel, I was intrigued.

"Ooooooh shit Udias, hit that spot right there baby, shiiiiit!" I panted.

"You like this shit, baby?" He smacked my ass so hard, I felt it vibrate in my pussy.

"Oh, my gaaaawd, deeper daddy!"

"If I go any deeper, I'm gone, bust baby."

"Faster, then. Punish this pussy, please!" I screamed so loud it echoed off of the four walls surrounding us.

"Shhhh, baby you're gonna wake my daughter up!" He placed his hand over my mouth in an attempt to stifle my cries.

Rolling in my pussy, he made an effort to touch every sensitive spot there was in order to bring me to ecstasy. Oh, my gawd, I don't want this to end. I thrust my hips into his causing us to climax at the same time. He went to pull out of me, and I lifted my hips into his, and he exploded inside of me.

"Damn, that was good!" he said.

"It sure was," I crooned and kissed his emollient lips.

Grabbing my inner thigh, he squeezed. It felt so intensified that I felt wetness oozing down my middle taking me to another level of euphoria.

Jolting me out of my sleep, I realized I had been playing with my peach. My hands were sticky from the sex I thought I was having with the character visual I'd created in my head. Obviously, this was the best sex I'd had in a very long time. My pussy hadn't creamed this much in all the years I'd had sex with my husband.

Following a much-needed shower, I changed my bedsheets and laid back down to find myself fast asleep. Waking up to pack for my trip to Seattle, I felt a bit queasy. I shook it off and took a dose of Zofran before gathering the remainder of my things.

I'd signed up for a health and wealth conference as suggested by Trinh so that I could regain my footing as a divorcee. I'd always wanted to be successful in life and in business, and the conference offered an outlook on how to adequately do that.

On my way to the airport, I decided to pick up the phone to call someone I hadn't talked to in a few years. After ringing a few times, I was gonna hang up, then I heard the sweetest voice through the Bluetooth.

"Hello?" she paused.

"Aunt Junie, I miss you," a lone tear rolled down my left cheek. It was great to hear such a loving voice.

"Oh, my Lord. Bucky, come, it's Sugar Bear!" she yelled excitedly.

"This is a really fucked up scene. How could a human being be so animalistic?" Ojun quizzed rhetorically.

"I don't know," Jones shook his head. "When I got here, the boy had already expired, being that he was decapitated, but the dad was still alive. I kneeled down to check his pulse, he opened his eyes and saved me from being killed with a stifled scream. The perp charged toward me from the hallway but not before I was able to pull my piece and light his ass up." Bo informed me.

"Oh, damn. Here comes Internal Affairs." I said in all seriousness.

"I don't give a fuck. The perp was nutty enough to beat the first trial on insanity, escape the psychiatric hospital, then kill these innocent people and try to kill me. The father was a decorated navy seal a pillar in his community. The boy was fourteen, just starting high school, and already a varsity linebacker. I can't say I regret killing the crazy muthafucka before he had a chance to take me out," Bo responded.

"Why had you gone in before clearing the perimeter anyway?" I asked curiously.

"The neighbors all stood outside sobbing. They were saying that they'd heard blood-curdling screams and once I made it to the sliding door in the backyard, I noticed the boy's body on the sofa with his head on placed on the floor, facing him. I knew there wasn't anything that I could do for him, pulling my piece from the holster, I forged ahead. The kitchen had an entrance from three directions. I entered through one, checked the other, then as I rounded the kitchen island, I stepped in a puddle of blood.

I was inches away from the dad's body. I peeked through the other entrance and figured the coast was clear since I didn't see nor hear anything. Sliding my gun back in the holster, I checked for a pulse, and instinctively the victim's eyes popped open in freight. He used his last breath to mumble out a scream and tilt his head towards the suspect. His bravery and diligence saved my life," Officer Bo Jones smiled.

"Ah, the comradery of two servicemen makes me happy." I crossed my heart and lifted my hand to God.

I don't think I could've made it through this knowing that I'd lost a good friend of mine. Jones was one of the first guys I'd met when I took the job on the police force. He was the coolest cat there. While he was eight years my senior, he was very youthful. Married with three kids and a wealth of knowledge. I flocked to him like a moth to a flame, he was even a groomsman in my wedding. The bond we had was that of brothers. His wife and Ninny, may she rest in heaven, were good friends as well.

After the Medical Examiner's guys made it and picked up the bodies, we headed back to the station. Sitting there for a moment soaking today's events in, I thought about my late wife and child. The impact of grave loss took over my emotions, causing me to stand to my feet and pull my blinds closed. Being the lead detective in a small town had its perks, and having my own office was one of them.

"Baby, we're having a baby!" Ninny yelled as she jumped up and down, holding the EPT stick in her hand.

She tried to hand it to me, and I flinched, causing her to frown.

"What the hell is that, Jawaine? Were you not ready to be a daddy? You been busting nuts in me left and right so what the fuck did you think was gonna happen?" She pitched a fit and stormed out of the bathroom with me hot on her heels.

"Ninny, stop."

"No, if you didn't want a baby, you should've taken the initiative not to get me pregnant."

"Ninny, who said I didn't want a baby?"

"You just did," she yelled.

"Naw, I didn't say shit. You assumed I didn't want a baby. We are not gonna do that, Love."

"Well, you snatched away from the test."

"Yeah, I did. Not because I didn't want a baby, though."

"Well, why then?"

"Because," I paused in embarrassment.

"Because what, Jawaine?"

"Because you peed on it. I wasn't touching your pee."

Bursting into laughter, she had tears in her eyes. I didn't think the shit was funny, I felt like she was making a mockery of me.

"Really? You jumped back like it was acidic," she continued to laugh.

Finally, I decided to join her in laughter because it was pretty hilarious. Of course, I didn't see my facial expression, but it had to be pretty mean since it hurt her feelings. Although I joined her in hilarity at my expense, I felt like shit for the way I reacted. I picked her up and spun her around before placing her on the bed.

With tears in her eyes, she looked me square in the face and asked, "Are you ready to raise a child?"

Knock. Knock.

The knock on my office door broke me from the happy but painful memory of my beautiful late wife. Had I sat any longer stewing, I may have shed a tear or two. Standing to my feet, I moseyed toward the door. I pulled it open and there stood my guys.

"Hey, we were gonna head out to wind down at the pool hall, you wanna join us?" Ojun quizzed.

"Yeah, let me grab my things," I responded.

I turned to grab my briefcase and files that I had been studying for a cold case I'd been working on. Stuffing them in the side pocket, I felt a hand on my shoulder. I didn't have to turn to know it was Bo.

"You good?" he asked.

"Not really. I'll be fine though; I think a night out with the guys will help me get through whatever I'm going through. It still feels like any day she's gonna come home and tell me she's okay."

"Yeah. I feel you; I can't imagine what you're going through, bro. But what I can say is, I'm here for you my dude. Any time of day or night, I'm right here."

"For sure." We slapped hands and headed out.

We shot a few games of pool, had a few beers, and talked a lot of shit. They snuck one in on me. The truth was they'd gotten me out of my element to celebrate the release of my new book.

"So, Jawaine…" Ojun announced.

"What, bruh?" I responded.

"Is your next book gonna be some gruesome shit like we deal with every day or will it be another loooove story." He dragged the words, and air quoted them. Everyone laughed at my expense.

"My loooove story hit number one on the charts, though." I laughed.

"He ain't lying. The whole damn department and their mamas bought books," Bo chimed in.

We shot the shit for a little while longer, had a few more drinks, then headed home. I had to pack. A friend of mine, Sabrina Jenkins, author of *Tricked By All*, invited me to be a guest speaker at her conference, so I had a long day ahead of me.

"I'd like to introduce you to my good friend. He's a decorated detective, a widow, and a business owner. He has loved, lost, and recuperated. Author of True Love Never Dies, Prodigal Son."

"Thank you, ladies and gentlemen. I feel quite honored to be up here today to share my road to wealth and mental health.

Nodding my head at the crowd, I was consumed by an overwhelming cloud of necessity to teach, to give, and to free myself of a story I'd never verbally told to anyone.

"My journey started back when I was nine years old. I met the love of my life when I moved into a house right next door to her. My mother Janice and the man that I knew as my dad, Jeff, was murdered by my biological father, Dawaine, in my presence. From what my adopted mom told me was that Dawaine had asked to meet up so that we could get to know each other, and she'd encouraged them to oblige his request.

Once we arrived, Dawaine shook my hand, attempted to grab my mother's bottom, and stuck his tongue out being very disrespectful. Jeff asked him to keep his hands to himself. He'd warned him that if he didn't, that day would be the last day he'd see me or my mother. He chilled out, still lusting after my mother and paying me little attention. For a moment, I thought everything was gonna continue smoothly.

After the initial introduction, Dawaine had obviously forgotten the purpose of the visit. He'd gotten so aggressive with my mom that my dad stepped in and told my mother and me to get into the car. As we did as we were told, my dad and Dawaine broke into a scuffle, and of course, my dad had the upper hand on him. Dawaine took the coward way out, he pulled a knife from his boot and stabbed dad in the shoulder. My mother wasn't having it, though. She ran to his aid with me on her heels, and wilded out. I mean she hit Dawaine with some mean hooks.

Dawaine supposedly waved the hypothetical white flag. They let up off of him, and we all headed back to the car. Before making it there, I heard fireworks, which is what I now recognize as gunfire. It hit my dad in the head, killing him on impact. Dawaine walked over to my mother and reached his hand out to her, but she refused to let Jeff go. He yelled to her that if she didn't leave with him, she'd die too.

Turning to him with disdain in her eyes, she gritted for him to go ahead and take her out. Without a second thought, he looked me in the eye and pulled the trigger, also shooting her in the head." I paused, finally focusing on the crowd before me who were all dabbing the corners of their eyes.

"I do apologize to you all, I seemed to have gotten off track. Sabrina, I apologize for doing this to your audience."

"You're good, love. Continue."

"I really got off track. I only attempted to give you guys a little bit of the struggle before the strength. I needed you to know where my mental health was before this journey, I had to check out before I checked in. I wouldn't date anyone partly because I was deathly afraid of a lunatic like my father taking both our lives. Not knowing what happened to him after he escaped also had me on edge for many years. Come to find out someone found him in a crack house with his eyes dug out of his head.

Moving on. That is a few pieces of my past that made the whole man you see here today. I had a great life. My mother's best friend, Huang, raised me as her own even though she and her husband are Vietnamese. To this day, I call them mom and pop. Bao, my Pop was the lightweight boxing champion. He taught me everything I needed to know about being a man and a husband. Of course, I was teased throughout school for having Vietnamese parents, and I had to fight like crazy." I shook my head as a smile graced my face.

"My very first fight was with a guy in the eighth grade. I had the hugest crush on my neighbor who was also my best friend, but she had a crush on him, and he paid her no mind because she wasn't fast like the girls our age. He was after a certain girl for the prom, but I made sure I beat him to the punch and asked her to accompany me. The following week he and two of his friends cornered me in the bathroom at school.

They'd assumed I couldn't fight because my Pop was Asian. At least that's what they were telling one another. My best friend's uncle and my Pop had taught me several things about how to hold my own. Not only did I have to protect myself, but I also had to protect my best friend. Needless to say, I kicked their asses and won the girl. Am I proud of that today? No. Was it a part of my Journey? You bet your ass it was.

Let's fast forward to junior year in college. I didn't have many problems being that I was a star wide receiver, but I found myself deeper in love with the young woman who still kept me in the gray area or friend zone, I might say. She'd finally won the guy from eighth grade during our sophomore year of high school, and I was broken. I would get girls just to try to make her jealous, but none of it worked.

One night after a huge argument between us, she stormed off with her boyfriend, and we'd both ended up at the same party. It was then I figured, I should let go of any possibilities between us. That night, I met the woman who would later become my wife and mother of my child.

My best friend and I once spoke on a regular basis, randomly those regular phone calls became a rarity, and ended up being a surprised to hear from you. While I always loved her, I freed my heart up for my wife to take hostage." I smiled in remembrance of her little booty twerking. She decided to give me a lap dance for my birthday, and it was amazing.

"Well, I ended up being with her for almost nine years before her life was taken by a couple of crackheads looking for a fix. That was a hard time for me as I not only lost my wife but also my unborn child. She had less than six weeks until her actual due date. I went from being drunk in love to actually being drunk and unable to face the next minute of the day.

The one thing that held me up was the fact that I knew if God brought me to it, He'd bring me through it. My parents were definitely my rocks. Them, my Uncle Bucky, and my Aunt Junie, the neighbors and my parents' best friends, helped me tremendously. The only piece missing from that was my best friend. I hoped she'd show up in the four months it took me to face the world again, but she never did. I was so upset that she hadn't, I swore on my wife and child that I'd never forgive her.

With her and I being raised together, I'm sure she knew that's how I felt, so in the years she never reached out, I charged it to her assuming I wouldn't accept her apology. Maybe a few years ago, I wouldn't have accepted any excuse, but the man I am today has room in his heart for forgiveness. I forgave her a long time ago.

My full autobiography is on my website, www.prodigalson2019.net if you 'd like to read more about my story. This session pretty much wraps up my health, and unfortunately, it also wraps up my time. Needless to say, I didn't get around to discussing my businesses and how they came to fruition. If you're ever in Milwaukee, please don't hesitate to stop by my art gallery Ninny's Point of View and my restaurant Jay's Soul Food and Seafood. Thank you all for listening to my health journey and if you haven't read my book, *True Love Never Dies*, it's available on Amazon, on my website, and I'll stick around to autograph copies."

The end of the Health and Wealth conference came as quickly as my forty-five-segment ended. I'd been in my own world thinking of how my better speech could've been, and how much more informative it should've been, when I felt a hand touch my elbow.

"Excuse me, sir, before you leave for the night, do you mind signing a book for one of your biggest fans?" a sweet voice sang out.

Turning around to face the woman whose familiar voice held my next breath captive; I couldn't believe my eyes. I had to pinch myself because I was in utter disbelief. Sweeping her off her feet, I spun her around and kissed her the top of her head for old time's sake. It was her; *she* was here at the conference and heard my story. After placing her back on her feet, we stood there both breathless and speechless, taking in each other's presence.

"Wow, of all the people in the world, I didn't expect to see you here. What are you doing in Seattle, and when the hell did you become Mr. Articulate?" I smiled, punching Jawaine's arm.

"Ouch, I see you done gained a little strength, that hurt a lil bit. I wrote a book about being in love, my editor is the articulate one." We laughed as he rubbed his arm in the spot, I'd hit him.

"Stop being a wuss, it wasn't that hard."

"You look great KeKe. What brings you to Seattle?" He asked as he looked me up and down, obviously taking in the weight gain.

I was already subconscious about my heaviness, and he wasn't making me feel any better. Although he said I'd looked great, I felt like I could use a little work to get the thickness in all the right places.

"Thanks, you don't look too bad yourself. You almost look like the character visual of the main character in your book," I smiled.

Taking in his masculine chocolate frame, I had to remember that my divorce was still pending. Knowing Jon, he probably had me trailed to try and get me for spousal support. I looked around to see if I'd noticed anyone who may have been taking pictures of me, but found nothing. I knew it had to be the primal fear of my broken marriage and known actions of a vindictive soon-to-be ex-husband.

"Are you okay?" Jawaine quizzed with a risen eyebrow.

"Yeah, I'm good. It's so much has happened can we go somewhere and talk?"

"Sure. Let me finish breaking down my table, and I can meet you at the restaurant near the corner. Where are you staying?" He quizzed.

"I'm here at the Executive Inn. I chose this spot because it's near the Space Needle."

"You don't say... I'm here too. I'm touring tomorrow." He smiled.

"Well, you wanna put your things away and meet me for dinner at Brella's?"

"I'm not really a burger menu only type of man, I need hearty food," he rubbed his stomach. "I've heard great things about Trace, let's try that out. There are burgers there if that's what you really want." He offered.

"No problem, Prodigal Son, I'll go to my room and change I'm in 318. Stop by when you're ready." I responded.

Jawaine always did like food. When we were younger, I'd go to his house, and he'd literally be eating then we'd walk the few steps to my house, and he'd be all up in Aunt Junie's pots. She'd never scold him for it though, all she would do is ask if he'd washed his hands. She loved herself some him. By the time Jawaine had shown up, I'd taken a shower and changed into camouflage joggers and matching shirt set. He knocked on the door, and my heart pounded out of my chest to a beat of its own.

"Calm down Ken, it's just Jawaine. Your best friend, remember him?" I coached myself as I walked to the entrance.

Pulling the steel door open, he matched my fly. Rocking a pair of black and grey camouflage joggers with a black t-shirt to match, he looked like fine chocolate that I definitely would want a taste of. *Damn he got fine over the years,* I thought.

Had he not lifted my chin with his hand, I wouldn't have noticed the fact that my mouth was agape.

"The only thing missing is a string of drool. You need some water, Bestie? Your mouth been open since you opened the door."

"Shut up, crazy. Step in while I grab my clutch."

"No problem," he responded.

I put a little extra sway in my hips because I knew he was watching. Purposely dropping one of the Lana yellow gold hoops I had clutched my hand, I stopped abruptly bending in front of him. As I thought, he was so into watching my ass, he ran straight into it. When he wrapped his hands around my waist, every synapse in my brain had to fire to keep me from backing this ass up.

"Shit, girl. Be careful." He said, and his gaze held me there longer. "This picture is pretty dope," he said.

"Me? You walked into me because you were so busy watching my ass that you didn't know I stopped."

"Ha. Is that what you think?"

"Nope, that's what I know. We both know you weren't that into a painting of a damn bush," I laughed. "You own an art gallery, so I'm sure you have an eye for real pieces."

"I guess I'm busted," he smirked sexily.

After a few minutes of flirtatious repartee, we headed to the elevator. I stood in front of him, leaving him to feel the need to lean over my shoulder to hit the L button indicating we needed the lobby.

"Damn, KeKe."

"What?" I tittered nervously.

"Your scent is inviting, what is it?

Biting my tongue, I took in Jay's presence because I didn't know when the next time would be that I'd see him. I inhaled deeply taking in the Gucci Guilty cologne. I knew exactly what it was because I'd bought it for him on plenty of birthdays.

"It's called Flirt, It's actually a shower gel, not a perfume."

"I'm gonna step on the other side, okay?" He responded.

I had attended a Pure Romance party that one of the football wives had thrown, it was there that I'd bought the flirt because of a familiarity game we played. The purpose of the game was to familiarize us with the products and the benefits of them. Although there were very interesting devices, I wasn't into toys. I always purchased things like shower gel, lingerie, lubricant, and fragrances.

On top of being a shopaholic, the prices were very reasonable. When I shopped at www.thepinkdoll.com, I'd spend whatever was necessary with Rinata simply because she was an amazing host and had earned my loyalty.

"You good?"

"When did you become so lax?" Jawaine quizzed.

"What do you mean?" I ogled him, confused.

"You're different."

"Just like you, I been through a lot. You don't know the half."

"Sounds like we should've gone to happy hour."

"Well, it's not too late."

With that being said, we rerouted to the bar ate chips a dip and had several drinks. After I started feeling myself, I invited Jawaine up to my room. The inebriated me shoved the logical me into a dark hole and closed the lid. The last thing I remember was the drunken dark angel saying, have fun girl, fuck Jon! Jon who?

"Well, it was a lot I dealt with after I allowed Jon to cut me off from everyone. After that, everything went downhill in our marriage. He knew I'd essentially allowed him to cause me to alienate myself from everyone. Thus, he took full control of the marriage and me because I was so into being his wife, I was blinded to his cruel intentions," Kenleigh said before sipping more of her Mai Tai.

"Damn, KeKe. I knew it was bad, but I had no idea things were horrible." I admitted.

"Oh, you have no idea." She half-smiled, and it broke my heart.

"Please, enlighten me."

"Where do I start?"

"From the beginning, I have all night."

"Well," she started. "First, I want to apologize for being so into him that I wasn't there for you during your darkest hours. You were always there for me when I needed you," she smiled sheepishly.

"What's that?" I chuckled.

"I remember one night I called you, and I knew you were fucking, but you got up out of the pussy and came to my aid."

"When did you get the sailor's mouth?" I quizzed.

"After I started visiting my mom in prison, I found my voice. That's another story, though," she smiled.

"Well, maybe if my friend wants to be my friend again, we can talk about it one day."

"We sure will talk more about Trinh. She's a mess, worse than Aunt Junie, you'd like her. Anyway, I've been pregnant three times, and I'm not a mother. I've had three fractured ribs, two black eyes, shared my bed with a pregnant side chick, and to top it off, stepmother to two love children and one on the way." She took a deep breath to seemingly keep her tear-welled eyes from spilling over.

"Wow," I reached for her hand. Surprisingly she moved it out of my grasp, so I slid my hand back into my personal space. "My bad, I'm here for you, love."

"It's cool. I know if I allow your empathy, the waterworks would start, and 've cried enough tears for that bastard."

"Understood. You want to talk about your journey to our meeting today? What made you say I've had enough?

"Were you not listening?" she laughed. "Three miscarriages, two were eaten out of me, and one stressed out of me. Physical, mental, and emotional abuse. Three baby mommas, one of which I had to share my damn bed." She shook her head, fervently. "The bastard had her under the impression that I couldn't carry baby to term and had me under the impression that she didn't have anywhere to go and no family."

"How did he... What made him... How was she ever allowed inside of your home in order for you to accept her into your bed?"

Placing her hands over her beautiful face, she swiped her hair behind her ear, which revealed a scar on her forehead. I would be sure to question her about that. This muthafucka had lost his damn mind.

"I allowed him to invite her in for a threesome. After I found out he was still sleeping with her, she became a part of our sexual routine, and before I knew it, the bitch had moved herself and her grocery bag full of clothes into our home, fired our housekeeper, and was sleeping on the opposite side of him in our bed." Her shoulder shrug was nonchalant, it made it seem like she believed the behavior to be normal.

"Okay. I know there's nothing I can say to make you feel good, bad, or indifferent. I just wish I could've been there for you. I love you bestie, I always have."

"Yeah, I know. I've always loved you, too," she responded.

"I'm buzzing. I need some sleep."

As if on cue, our waitress walked up to our table to ask us if we needed anything else. I picked up the check then we headed out to the elevator. Once inside of the elevator, I hit the button for our floor and stood back into the corner.

"You mighty quiet over there."

I lifted my head from its resting position on the wall of the elevator. "Yeah, I don't want to cross any lines with your fine ass. I don't wanna take advantage of a damsel in distress," I smirked.

"I am no longer in distress, but I'm a fine ass damsel if I must say so myself." Kenleigh sauntered over to me, backed her ass up against my front, then leaned back into my chest.

"See, why you playing with the kid?"

"Who said I was playing?"

"Listen, you don't want this thug right here," I ground my woody into her.

The elevator door opened, and we exited. In route to her room, I attempted to calm my erection by putting my hand in my pocket. I rubbed the inside of my thigh which usually worked but tonight, looking at Kenleigh's thick thighs and wide hips, Lord have mercy on my soul. Help me, Jesus. I'm gonna need the father, son, and the holy spirit to keep me from blowing her back out tonight.

We made it to her door, and she slid her key card to enter her room. I stood back, not wanting to violate our friendship, because I didn't feel right knowing that she'd just poured salt on open wounds. I wasn't an opportunist and was in no shape or form into fucking without feeling. I would turn thirty in a few weeks and ready to settle down.

"You wanna come in for a minute?" KeKe asked.

"Nah, I'mma go head to my room before–"

She snatched her top off, revealing the perfect set of double ds'. She was tatted up under her shirt. Her beautiful skin revealed three sets of footprints lined across the left side of her chest, Chinese lettering between her boobs, and four butterflies up her right side that revealed the names of both her parents, and Uncle Bucky and Aunt Junie. I couldn't say that shit didn't turn me on all over again.

Kenleigh bit her bottom lip seductively then beckoned her finger for me to cross the threshold. I threw caution to the wind and followed her lead. The door slammed shut, and she rushed me. Our lips locked and we indulged in passionate kisses. I grabbed her neck, pushing her back to the wall to stare into her beautiful eyes. She pushed me roughly into the opposite wall and kissed my neck then my shoulders from collarbone to collarbone.

I leaned in, kissing her along her cheek line, and she held onto my broad shoulders. Grabbing her titties in either hand and squeezing them, her nipples broke free from the bra. Her areolas were beautifully chocolate, and I had to taste them. I leaned in and flicked my tongue across one, sending her into a frenzy. She purred and leaned her head back, exposing her neck. Kissing from her right shoulder to her ear, she started to tremble. Kenleigh grabbed me around my neck, essentially jumping into my arms and wrapping her legs around my waist, we headed to the bed in a heated exchange.

Slamming her onto the bed, I ripped my shirt off, then freed her from her joggers. Damn, she was thick as fuck. I knew I was gonna beat her pussy out the frame. I kissed her leg from behind her knee to her inner thigh near her mound. Her middle had visibly soaked through her panties. I took my two fingers and rubbed up and down her fat pussy lips then slid one of my fingers inside.

Even her moan was sexy, got damn. I stuck my finger in my mouth to suck her juices off. "Damn girl, your pussy taste like the protein I need to get through my day." I smiled down on her.

"Fuck me then, and stop talking."

Just I went to strip down to my boxers, my wedding band twinkled, in turn, causing me to stare at hers.

"What are you waiting on Jawaine? You got my pussy hot, don't back out now." She panted.

"I can't. I'm not a homewrecker, and I'm no one's side piece. I gotta go!" I grabbed my shit and headed to my room.

I tossed and turned all night long, thinking about how I might have blown my chances with my lifelong crush. Standing to my feet, I decided to get my hygiene out of the way so I could start my day. I'd set up a tour of Seattle, top of the list was the Space Needle. I'd been wanting to see it in person since watching

Grey's Anatomy with my mom. She was gonna be psyched when I brought her the Space Needle replica that I'd seen on the website. As much as my parents traveled, they'd never been here, surprisingly.

After I finished everything, I stepped out of the room in route to my mapped-out day. I was standing at the elevator when my phone chimed. I looked down at the screen, and it was a message from Kenleigh.

KeKe: Do you want a friend to accompany you on your excursion today?

Message received 8:42 am

Instead of responding, I went down to her room and knocked on the door. I heard the latch opening, and there she stood just as beautiful as she had always been wearing a peach and mint green maxi dress. Coincidentally, I donned a tan and mint button down with tan shorts and mint Bally Marina's on my feet.

"Great minds think alike, I see," she said.

"Nah, great minds think for themselves, love."

"I can dig it. Come in, let me grab my clutch. Have you eaten breakfast?"

"No. I was gonna grab something on the way out," I spoke from the hall leading into the room.

"I have fruit and bagels if you want any of it."

I decided to go into the openness of the room and grab a banana. I was gonna buy a breakfast sandwich, but this was healthier. I'd made the call to my parents while waiting on Kenleigh to finish whatever she was doing before stepping out. I'd told them that she was at the conference and they were ecstatic. I ended the call with I love you and we headed out to tour the city.

Some time into our day, Kenleigh got lightheaded, and we sat down on a bench. She said she'd been feeling sick for a while, but she paid it no mind.

"Are you pregnant?" I asked.

"If I am, I'm at least two months along because we hadn't had sex in roughly seven weeks. However, I've had my cycle, so I don't think so."

After sitting and talking for a while, I learned a lot more information. Kenleigh had petitioned Jon for a divorce, rented a condo and was living on her own, and was actually in contact with everyone that he had taken her away from. Her relationship with her mother had flourished over the years, and that made my heart smile. I was genuinely happy for her, and that was my word.

Standing to our feet, I took notice of the time and realized we'd sat and talked for two hours. Our tour of the Space Needle was in twenty minutes, so we decided to walk over to the landmark. We enjoyed each other's company and ended up at the corner store, buying a pregnancy test. After much persuasion and to her dismay, we did it anyway and were in my room waiting on results.

"Listen, walking back and forth isn't going to make time pass," I scolded.

"Neither is watching the seconds pass on your phone's timer, but has that stopped you from doing it?" she replied spunkily.

"Look Boo, you can slow up with that attitude. I was simply stating the obvious from my observation."

"Sorry," she whispered.

The timer went off, and we both ran into the bathroom to look at the EPT stick. The results were clearly what she knew they would be. Falling into my arms, she wept as I kissed her head and reassured her that everything would be alright.

Three weeks later…

Kenleigh (We)

"Yeah, I don't want to tell him about the baby though, Aunt Junie."

"It would be against everything you ever believed in, Sugar Bear."

"I know. But I don't want to," I pouted like a child.

There was dead silence on the line. In the next few moments, the only thing that could be heard was us breathing. I knew I was in deep thought and could only assume Aunt Junie was too. I had to tell Jon that I was pregnant, but I would tell him on my time, not anyone else's. I heard her stirring a pot, and my mouth began to salivate thinking of what it was she was cooking.

"Aunt Junie?"

"Yes, Sugar Bear?"

"What are you cooking?"

"You don't want to know," she laughed.

I could only assume she said that because she was cooking something, I'd drive three hours southwest of where I lived to have a taste. I could smell it in my sinuses, I knew it was goulash.

"Does it have corn, ham, sausage, shrimp, okra, and tomatoes in it?"

"Um…" she hesitated. "Don't you get your butt on that road. I'll come up to visit and make you some to put in the freezer."

"I'm on my way," I hung up. I knew I had to move fast before she contested my decision.

I grabbed a few clothes and threw them into a small overnight bag. Before I could finish loading the car, my phone rang, and I slid my finger across the screen without looking at the caller ID.

"Aunt Junie, I promise I'll be careful."

"I miss you, baby."

I looked at my screen, confused at the deep baritone voice in my ear.

"What do you want, Jon?"

"It's been over a month, and you haven't called me. I get it, Ken. You can ome home now."

"What the fuck you mean, Jon? I am home, and I'm busy, so if you're done, was headed to see my aunt and uncle."

"I'm not done, I'll never be done. You're my wife, and I'm not losing you ver a simple mistake. How many times do I have to apologize to you, baby?"

"How many times do I have to tell you I don't give a fuck about another mpty ass apology. That shit is whack and weak. I fell for your bullshit year after ear, side bitch after side bitch, and love child after love child. I'm not the simple rained bitch who allowed you to control her thoughts. Fuck you, Jonathan. Get e fuck off my line."

"I'mma let you—"

Before he could finish his statement, I'd disconnected the line on his ass. I asn't' trying to hear all his extra. Our whole relationship was built off of my eakness. Sometimes, I felt like I was the main chick that was really the side nick.

I gathered myself before pulling off. Needing to relax, I decided to switch y cd player to *10 Seconds* by Jazmine Sullivan. I didn't know what it was about er voice, but she would always get me through rough times. I rode and sang her ongs to the top of my lungs, and before I knew it, I was pulling into the driveway f my childhood home.

Sitting in the car for a moment, I looked around the cul-de-sac and reflected n the years I'd spent here. I peered from yard to yard and home to home, allowing y mind to engage in different memories. I had a load of emotions coursing rough my brain, to say it was overwhelming was an understatement.

The flashbacks were both happy and sad. I almost felt like I was losing my amn mind. Smiling at the last memory of ripping Jawaine's clothes off in his arents' house, I felt the seat of my panties get soaked. I leaned my head back gainst the headrest and allowed my hormones to take control of me. Before I new it, I was sticky and needed a shower. I had to laugh at myself, Jawaine had denied me sex twice, and here I was in my car having orgasmic remembrances of our lips locking.

I took a deep breath to gather myself, washed my hands with the sanitizer in my purse, wiped my juice box and thighs off with summer's eve wipes, then exited my vehicle. My legs were a wobbly, it was like I had been fucked like I was ugly. I couldn't believe I had taken myself to heights unknown off of two kisses and a finger from my best friend. I didn't want to think where my mind would take me after he laid that monster down that's hidden in his boxer shorts.

"Kenleigh," A voice called after me.

What the fuck was she doing calling my name? I know she don't think we're friends. She can't be that fucked up in the head. After hearing footsteps rapidly approach me, I braced myself in preparation for a fight and turned around to face my enemy.

"What's up, LaShay?" I grilled her with the meanest stare I could muster up.

"Whoa," she threw her hands up. "I was only coming to talk to you. I was visiting my parents and as I was leaving, I noticed you getting out of your car."

"Well, you can talk. What's up?"

"I've had time to reflect over the last few years, and I realized what I did to you was selfish and heartless. Every black eye I wore hidden underneath concealer and every bruise on my neck covered by turtlenecks, I deserved. Mama told me that God would never send me another woman's man, but I didn't understand until a few years ago."

"Your point?" I shrugged haphazardly.

"My point is I was young and dumb. I thought Jon would see that he belonged with me once I got pregnant. Instead, he beat my ass and tried to kick me in the stomach to make me miscarry," she admitted.

"Well, I guess sex doesn't make them love you and babies don't make them stay, huh?"

"That was cruel. I'm only trying to apologize to you for my part in your anguish as Jon's girlfriend and wife."

"Your lips keep moving, but I haven't heard an apology once. It sounds to me like you are giving me your side of the story now that Jon is happy with someone else."

"What? No, he isn't. He called and told me you left him, and he was trying to straighten his life up to get you back. We aren't sex partners anymore and hadn't been for about two years now. We are happy co-parents, so we actually talk to one another."

"Good for you, congratulations," I kept my bitchy façade going. I really had no fucks to give nor any energy on old shit. Him, her, or their child were no longer my business. What happened with them was on them.

"Look, I'm sorry for the part I played in hurting you. As a woman, I would never wish to endure what you have with your husband. I'm engaged to a wonderful man, and I pray that God spares me the heartache."

"There it is. You've finally come to terms with your truth. The truth is, you had a coming to Jesus moment and wanted a clean slate so your union wouldn't be tainted by your wrongdoings. I wish you the best," I said.

"Take it easy, Ken, it was nice seeing you. You look amazing."

"Yep, have a great life LaShay."

I walked inside of my childhood home to find Aunt Junie, and Uncle Bucky cuddled up on the sofa watching my man Denzel Washington kick ass in *Equalizer 2*. Kissing them both on the cheek, I headed to the kitchen to find my bowl of food in the microwave waiting to be warmed and eaten.

It looks different in here. I thought as I looked around, waiting for the timer to count down on the microwave. As I paid closer attention, the appliances had been switched out to all black, including a double-door Frigidaire and a flat top range. The cabinetry had been changed to oak, and the countertops were marble with the same marble as a backsplash for the wall behind stove. "Okay, Aunt Junie, I see you boo!" I snapped my fingers three times.

"I'm glad you decided to spend a few days with us. I sure miss having my Sugar Bear around." Uncle Bucky hugged my neck.

"I missed you two so much. I feel like I missed out on a lot of things over the years."

"Yeah, baby," Aunt Junie breathed. "Yesterday is history, tomorrow is a mystery, and today is a gift; hence, the reason we call it present. We knew you'd come around eventually, not saying we weren't butthurt that you dropped us like hot cakes, but we prayed every day for God to send His only begotten son to save you before one of us exited this life."

"Junie, stop being dramatic. We are healthy as oxen. The girl already learned her lesson. She don't need to leave here thinking we damn near dying, hell."

"Shut up, Bucky. I was talking to Sugar Bear."

"I see not much has changed between you two." I laughed.

"Nope, nothing but how much we love each other," Aunt Junie corrected me.

"I love y'all." I kissed their cheeks and headed out.

Once I made it to the interstate in route back to my residence, I decided to call Jawaine.

"Siri, call Sexstie," I said aloud.

"Calling Sexstie," Siri responded.

"Yo?" he answered.

"What you up to?"

"Chilling with my guys at the pool hall. What are you up to?"

"Just leaving Alabama, needed some goulash."

"Aunt Junie cooked my favorite and didn't invite a brother?" he laughed.

"Your ass is still greedy, huh?"

"Yep."

"I can call you back, I didn't wanna disrupt your guy's night out."

"It's all good, I see these clowns almost every day," He responded.

"Clowns?" I heard a few guys repeat.

"Yep, none of y'all wanna fight about it," Jawaine laughed. "Ouch, I was just kidding."

"I guess they did wanna fight, huh?" I laughed.

"Aye, I'mma step out so I can take this call. I'll be right back," he spoke to his homeboys.

"Hurry up, bruh. You up next," I heard someone say.

"Man, Bo, take my shot. I'm tryna talk to my best friend. Is that okay, fellas?"

"Nah, you know what, just call me back when you leave the pool hall. I don't want them to hate me before they meet me."

"Meet you?" Jawaine quizzed.

"Yeah, they'll meet me one day, right?"

"Well, I guess so."

"Love you, Bestie."

"Later, love you more."

As much as I dreaded to make my next phone call, I knew it was inevitable so I might as well had skedaddled along and got the shit behind me.

"Siri, call Piece of Shit."

"Calling Piece of Shit," Siri responded in a vernacular that was hell of funny.

"Hello," Jon answered.

"Hey, I need you to know that I'm nine weeks pregnant and I'm keeping my baby."

"I wouldn't ask you to kill it, Ken. It gives us a chance to work on us, I signed up for counseling, and I've been attending faithfully. I promise I will be the husband and father that I should be to you and our child."

"Jon, please. Stop, okay? All I want you to do is be a father to our child. I can't and won't deny that you're a great parent to your other kids."

"Ken, I'm learning how to be a better person, for you," he admitted.

"You won't be successful if you're doing it for me, Jon. Unless you want to change for you, your time is being wasted. Until you want to be a better you, the shit you're doing to correct the old you will never be mended at the core it will only polish the surface."

"Yeah Ken, I hear you. Haven't I taught you a lot?"

"Yeah, you did. You taught me how to take a punch, accept verbal abuse, belittle myself, and how to feel sorry for myself.

"That's not true Ken, and you know it!"

"The first step to recovery is admission. I had to admit to myself that I allowed you to do those things to me. The only thing that may continue is what we allow to happen. The saddest thing for me to admit learning from you. However, was that you taught me to recognize the gestures of hate and the language of evil. I know how to pick those two things out of an array of colors. Thank you for that, baby father."

"I'm not sure what you want from me, Kenleigh."

"All I want is you to be as good a father to our child as you are to your other children."

"I can do that Kenleigh, but I'm not giving up on us."

Jawaine (We)

I got so lifted the other night, I didn't remember to call Kenleigh back. The next day I spent time at the gravesite with my wife and child. After leaving there, I lacked the energy it took to focus and didn't want to talk to anyone. I'd been knee deep in work and thought about calling her today when my desk phone rang.

"Detective Li," I spoke.

"Hey, you. You avoiding me now?"

"Hell nawl, why would I do that?"

"I don't know. You tell me, love."

"Oh, you being funny huh, KeKe? Tryna sound like me on the phone. Why didn't you hit my cell?"

"Oh, but I did... several times my dude."

"Lies. My celly is right here, and I don't... oh!"

"Un-huh. So, tell me again that I hadn't hit your cell."

"Okay, my bad sexy... I mean bestie," I laughed.

"Oh, that's what we doing now? You playing with my emotions these days? I see how you do me. Anyway, I wanna come visit when I visit Trinh. Would that be okay?"

"Uh, yeah. Only thing is, I wouldn't be comfortable having you in my home. I still have pictures of my wife everywhere, the nursery is the same as it was, and it's just not welcoming to a woman right now."

"That's fine, do you know if they host Air BnB's in your area?"

"Yeah. There's a few on my street actually."

"Would you be willing to stay in one with me while I'm there or is that asking too much?"

"Yeah as long as you don't try to rape me or nothing. I know you want the kid bad like a heartbeat," I laughed.

We laughed and talked for some time before I was called out to help one of my guys with a crime scene investigation. When I got there, it had to be the most horrific scene I'd seen in a long time. It was a triple homicide that included a man, a pregnant woman, and a toddler. And apparently, the female murderer couldn't live with her decision because she killed herself in the den of the home.

Of course, scenes like this always remind me of Ninny and our unborn child. Any time I would work a scene of such caliber, I'd have to walk off to take a breather. You wouldn't believe the amount of cases in general that involve pregnant women and children. It saddens me to know such cruelty lies in the soul of a human being.

We worked the scene, collected our evidence, questioned bystanders as to what they may have heard if anything. From what was understood was the murderer was an ex-wife. They had adult children together, and she'd been creeping over to the victims' home whenever the wife was out of town, which was often. Apparently, he was supposed to remarry her but married the current wife last month much to the ex-wife's dismay and surprise.

The neighbors said they all were arguing on the lawn yesterday. The ex-wife ran her car into both the vehicles and fled the scene. A police report was made but sadly under false pretenses because when they looked into it, it was reported as an unknown vehicle and an unknown suspect. Here we are today with everyone dead, including the child who laid in her crib with blood and dried tear stains on her face.

After today's events, I decided to go home, shower, kick my feet up, and enjoy a shot or three of Gold Schlager. It had become one of my pastimes after a long night. It helped me to relax.

My phone rang jolting me out of my apparent doze. I looked at my caller id and recognized the number as the lady who owned the air bed and breakfast two doors down from my house. "Damn, it's only 8:56. I was already out for the count." I mumbled.

"Hello?"

"Hi, I was returning a phone call in reference to my rental property on Junic Way. Is Jawaine Li available?"

"Yes, ma'am, speaking."

"I'm sorry, did I catch you at a bad time? I realize Hawaii is five hours behind Milwaukee."

"No, ma'am. I had a long day. I was watching television, and it ended up watching me," we laughed.

"I certainly understand. Well, the property is a four-bedroom, Victorian style home with two and a half baths. The master's bedroom features a garden tub and a separate walk-in shower. The other three rooms house two queen-sized beds and mirrored closets. The dining room is separate from the kitchen which sits off the den. The neighborhood is lined with pristine homes and well-manicured lawns."

"Ma'am, no disrespect to you. I am well aware of the neighborhood. I live a few houses down from your rental property. Long story short, I'm widowed, and I have a friend coming into town. My home is not ready for visitors. I'd like her to feel at home without being inside of my home."

"Understood. That's enough information. The deposit is four hundred fifty dollars, and the daily rate is one hundred thirty dollars per night. Are you a uniformed officer?"

"That's not too bad, I'll be paying for her. And do you mean military or police?"

"Either."

"Yes, ma'am, I'm a detective for Milwaukee police department. Why do you ask?"

"Great, I offer thirty percent discounts for uniformed officers, you're in luck. Thank you for your service. Will you be interested in the property, or are you merely shopping around?"

"I'm definitely going with you on the property, you have five-star ratings on Airbnb.com. I'll book online tonight; is there any way we can get confirmation delivered to both our email addresses?"

"Of course, when we hang up text me the second email and the dates, you'll be occupying so I can key it into my calendar. Unfortunately, that's the only way I can send it to two emails. The host I use doesn't offer duplicate confirmations at checkout. Thank you so much, sweetheart for doing business with me."

"No problem ma'am. I'll text you the second email right now and also pay for the house before someone snags the dates I need. I hope you enjoy Hawaii."

"I live here," she laughed. "I come home for two weeks to make sure my properties are taken care of every three months then head back to my beach house. I wouldn't have it any other way, son. Don't forget to check the uniformed officer box and provide your credentials so you are allowed the discount. I'll be in touch, enjoy your stay."

"Good evening, ma'am."

"Good night, sir."

"How was your flight?" I asked Kenleigh as I grabbed her roller luggage and placed it in my trunk.

"I've had better flights, but I won't complain. How are you?" she rebutted.

We got into my car and headed toward the house to wind down. I'd already been there making the place homely and to prepare dinner being that her flight was due to land so late in the evening.

"Dang, a sister didn't even get a hug or nothing. You can at least act happy to see me, jerk." She folded her arms in a bratty manner.

Tugging on her arm, I pulled her into my direction and kissed her cheek. "My bad, I was ready to get the hell out of the airport. My nerves still get bad when I'm in airport traffic, that hasn't changed, and I don't think it ever will."

"Forgiven, I guess," I recognized a smile tugging at the corner of her lips.

"Is that right?"

"Yep."

"Well, I guess you ain't getting no food then... I guess."

"Oooh Jawaine, what you cooked? We issssss hungry," she rubbed her belly, staring at me.

"I know your greedy ass ate."

"And did, but what that mean? I'm hungry as a bear coming out of hibernation."

The shit that came out of Kenleigh's mouth was unbelievable at times. The girl I remembered was shy and timid, but I guess that girl had dissipated along with our late teen and early twenty years. She was witty, beautiful, kind, intelligent, and no longer tied down. Jon was forced to sign the divorce papers by his lawyer had he not wanted his dirty laundry aired and his career ruined if things ended up in a nasty divorce.

"You'll see when we get there lil greedy. That baby gone be so fat, every time I talk to you, you got something in your damn mouth."

Kenleigh turned her face to the window and mumbled something under her breath. I don't know if what I thought I heard was what I heard, but I had to ask. It was worth the try.

"Whatchu said?" I hiked my eyebrow.

Turning to face me, she licked her full, plump, tasty lips and repeated herself. "I said. Hopefully, I'll have you in my mouth before I go back home."

She tilted her head from one side to the other like the man did on the *I was waiting on you at the door* video clip. I, for once in my life, was speechless. I swallowed hard as I turned the car into my neighborhood.

"Oh, the cat got your tongue. You quiet as hell over there big boy. What's good?" she reached over to rub my arm.

I stared at her, as I knew the glare in her beautiful orbs was begging for the wood. My only inhibition was she'd only had one dick in her life, and I knew once she got a taste of the kid it was over for her. She'd definitely be uprooting her life and moving to boring as Milwaukee to be near me. I wasn't ready to disrupt our friendship just yet. I wanted us to rekindle our companionship so that we'd be mutually beneficial to one another. I was far from the young man she knew all those years ago. I was a grown man with grown needs and fucking just wasn't gone cut it, neither would being a rebound.

"Is that apple pie I smell?" Kenleigh asked as soon as we entered the house.

"Yup. With crumble just like you like it."

"Oh my God, I could jump in your arms right now and kiss you all over your face. Thank you so much."

"I'll settle for a hug if you can behave yourself."

She smiled wickedly before walking over to me and enwrapped my waist. It reminded me so much of the olden days on her Aunt and Uncle's porch. I kissed her forehead, which always sealed the deal, notifying us that the hug was over. She looked at me with adoration in her dreamy orbs, and I felt like a new person.

"Can I have a slice of pie first?"

"As long as you wash your hands, you can have anything you want, baby."

We laughed at my spot-on attempt to channel Aunt Junie, voice and all. Every time I'd go over their house, and I smelled anything cooking, I'd ask if I could have whatever it was. Aunt Junie would hit me with the exact line. She was a huge part of my life and still is. I talk to her on the phone and on facetime as much as I talked to my mom. I was blessed to have such loving people to be a part of my upbringing.

We walked further into the house, and Kenleigh started to take in the small things I'd done to make the house a home for her. I had fresh flowers on both the coffee and dining table, I bought movies that weren't available on demand, got us a few games to play, and a few other minor things. The house was already beautiful, so it didn't need much.

After we ate dinner, she showered, and we sat at opposite ends of the sofa. She was glowing like a damn glow stick, it made me miss my wife even more.

"I'm so beat. It feels like my toes are throbbing inside of my socks."

"Let me see," I requested.

Kenleigh eyed me strangely as if the request I'd made was outside of the norm. It wasn't like I'd asked her to stand on the table and strip or to finger that fat pussy that's peeking through her pajama shorts, while I watched.

"Girl, give me ya damn feet, shit."

"Damn, you ain't gotta be so damn rude."

I patted my leg so she could put her feet up there. Finally, after a stare down and my handsome smirk she gave in. Grabbing her left foot, which was the furthest away, she attempted to move it out of my touch, but I had a vice grip on it. Starting at the arch of her foot, I used my thumbs to apply slight pressure by rotating them outwardly. The relaxation of her shoulders told me I was doing her right. Inch by inch, I made my way to the base of her toes and back down to the arch. After repeating that motion a few times, I held her ankle in one hand, grabbed a slight hold of her toes with the other and rotated her foot doing a little reflexology to her calf muscle. When I was finished with that leg, I repeated the job on the other.

"Oh my God, Jawaine," she gasped. "This feels so good. I could lay here and let you do this all night."

When I was done with my interpretation of reflexology, I grabbed Kenleigh's foot and kissed it. She shuddered at the touch of my lips on her feet. I had it in my mind to suck her toes, but I didn't want to send her ass over the edge. It was bad enough I was salivating at the sight of the fuzzy peach, struggling with containing the beast. It wasn't too many more times I would be able to let that pussy slide.

She turned around, laid her head in my lap on top of a pillow, and we tuned into Den of Thieves. Surprisingly, I had never watched the movie before. Being that I was a huge Gerard Butler fan, it was baffling. Ever since I'd become a detective, the only crime shows I'd shown any interest in was First 48, and that was a rarity. I massaged her scalp with my hand gently as she laid there, content. Not in a million years had I imagined the scene before me. I think I'm in love with my best friend– again.

Three months later...

"My boy got a strong heartbeat, don't he?" Jon's raggedy ass boasted. He'd been present at every turn of the pregnancy. Every time my obstetrician looked in my pussy, he was right there looking with him.

"Who said it was a boy?"

"His heartbeat is too strong to be a girl."

"Where do you get your logic?" I shook my head.

This dude was a straight clown, I sure knew how to pick them. The further I got into my pregnancy, the more I disliked his ass. I wanted to run away and never look back, but I wouldn't dare do that to my child. I couldn't be the mother that was so bitter that I deprived my child of a relationship with the man who was responsible for their being.

"That's what J. Buckley's wife said," I responded.

"How many sons does she have?"

"None."

"Nuff said," I ended with my point proven.

The door opened to the exam room and in walked Dr. Lamendola. He shook both our hands before grabbing a seat on the stool. Smiling brightly, he rolled up close to the bed and pulled out the printed off ultrasound pictures.

"Well, Mr. and Mrs. Freeman, great news, you are on the cusp of your second trimester and almost in the clear. Once we cross the threshold into month seven, we will all breathe much easier. You have a little over fifteen weeks left until delivery. The baby is developing well, did you want to know the gender?"

"Yes, sir," Jon responded.

"No, we don't wanna know. We know the baby is healthy and that's a great enough answer. One thing I do want you to know, however."

"What's that Mrs. Freeman?"

"I'm Ms. Peters now, we're divorced."

"Understood. Any questions, comments, or concerns?"

"Yes, sir. Is it true that when you are carrying a boy, the heart rate is higher when you hear it on the lil sonogram thingy?"

"You mean the doppler? No, not at all most fetal heartrates at this point in the pregnancy are roughly between one-hundred-ten to one-hundred-sixty regardless of the gender," he smiled.

"Well, what about the old wives tale of the stomach sitting high or sitting low?"

"Also, a myth."

"The only surefire way of finding out is to verify by ultrasound." He shook the paper in his hand. "Anything else?"

"No, Doc, I'm good. Of course, unless Mr. Doctor Quarterback over here is still learning about old sayings and whatnot."

"Nah, I'm good, Ms. Peters," Jon said with a slight attitude. That nigga acts like I gave a fuck if he was feeling some type of way.

"Okay, well I'll see you in a month and after that, every two weeks. Alrighty?"

"Okily dokily." I smiled.

Walking out of the clinic, people on the outside stared at us like we were the perfect couple. They had no idea what I put up with when I was Mrs. Jonathan Freeman. Had I still been wed to the jerk beside me that happens to be selling out his show, I wouldn't have made it this far along in my pregnancy. Yet there he was, holding doors and rubbing the small of my back like any good man would do for his pregnant wife.

"Why thank you, my good man," I mocked Spanky from the movie *Little Rascals*.

"Oh, you just a regular old comedian, huh?" Jon smiled.

It was the smile that I fell in love with. If I didn't know any better, I'd say the counseling was working in his favor. Too bad I'd fallen outta love with him a long time ago.

"You wanna go to dinner?" he asked.

"I don't see why we can't do dinner. Justine's?"

"Why did I know you'd want seafood?"

"You didn't, cuz I'm craving the red beans and rice platter with sausage." I stuck my tongue out at him.

"You are so beautiful. I promise I won't mess this up, Ken. Not this time around."

"It's dinner, Jon."

"Meet me there at 7:30, same table as always."

"I'll be there. Hopefully, you can remember which table ours is." I grilled.

"Don't ruin the moment," he leaned in to kiss me, but I gave him my cheek."

It was only noon, I had time to go home and relax before dinner with the jerk of the year. I dozed off, dreaming of Jawaine. He was giving me his signature massage, only this time, I donned a white robe with nothing underneath. Standing to my feet, I looked him directly into his lust-filled, sexy orbs then pulled the string on my robe. Before he could attack my boobs with his warm, tepid, succulent lips, my phone rang, juddering out of my sleep.

Not wanting to be bothered, I looked at the caller ID, and a smile crept across my face as I slid my finger over the screen.

"Hello?"

"Hey, sorry to wake you. Do you want me to call you back?"

"No, Jawaine, I'm woke now, silly. What's up?"

"I was calling to see how the appointment went."

"It went well, we can talk about it this weekend when I come out."

"I'm having dinner with Jon today."

I figured I'd put that out there so I could see how he'd react. Was it childish of me? Yes. I was feeling Jawaine, he treated me far better than Jon ever could, and it's only been a few months since we'd rekindled.

"Oh, ok."

"Huh?"

"I said, okay. Like Kenleigh, what else do you want me to say, love?"

"Nothing, I guess."

I was a little salty that he didn't say more. We had a great time together, I thought we were working on us, but to my surmise, we're back in the friend zone.

"Call me when you get back home so that I know you made it safe. Love you, bestie." He didn't give me a chance to respond before he disconnected the call. Had he given me the chance, he would've known I was already home.

I stared at my phone in disbelief, what the fuck did I just do? Sitting up in my bed, I scooted my bottom toward the pillows to lean my back against the headboard, once I was comfortable there, I laid my head in my hand and balled my eyes out. It had been a minute since I cried a good, soul-wrenching cry. I needed it.

"Thank you for coming, Ken."

"I'm a woman of my word, Jon. I always have been."

"Yes, that was one of the many qualities that I love about you. Even when we were younger, if you said you would, you did."

"I'd say it was one of my downfalls. Even with the handful of friends I did have, they took advantage of that part of me as well. Look at what LaShay did to me. Oh, did she tell you she apologized to me for sneaking with you behind my back?"

"Ken, when did we sneak behind your back? Me and LaShay's whole relationship was in your face like 3D. You chose to turn a blind eye to that," Jon said nonchalantly. "Let's get all this out on the table tonight. I bought you here to tell you that the things I did to you in our relationship were both of our faults. I did a lot of the shit I did, because you pretended to not recognize what was going on."

"You took advantage of me because you knew I loved you and would do anything for you. Let's get that out there, Jon."

"Yeah, even allow me to sleep with other hoes because you weren't ready to give up your virginity. I told you the night you decided to give me the pussy that I was fucking who I wanted to fuck, and you still took your ass to the hotel, rented a room, made it all pretty and feminine and allowed me to abuse you. You didn't even demand respect, Ken," he swirled the last of his drink and gulped it down.

The waitress was walking past us, and Jon stopped her for his fourth glass of D'usse cognac XO. He may have well ordered the whole bottle. His liquor was hitting, and he was finally laying down the law. Jon was giving me the lay of the land that he'd kept hidden when he was a cocaine using, cheating, physically abusive, bitch of a husband.

"I did. I allowed everything you put me through. I never thought I would come to terms with my truth, but here I stand. Every black eye, every broken bone, every fractured rib, and every loss of pregnancy was all on me. I accept my fault in it all. I accept that I tried to love a broken man," a lone tear escaped my eye, and the pain that I had been holding in, had finally been completely freed.

"I didn't bring you here to belittle you. You started this shit Ken, not me."

"Good night, Jon," I grabbed my things and walked away.

After leaving, the restaurant, I rode around in complete silence for a little while. There was absolutely no way I'd go home to sulk, so I took in the beautiful scenery the city had to offer. The skyline from the benches was beautifully set on the water like an expensive painting. A few hours had passed, and it was time I went home.

When I pulled into my driveway, a set of headlights whipped in behind me. With my job, I tried to keep my address private, so that people I caught cheating, or recipients my employees served wouldn't come for my head.

I pulled my pistol from my purse and exited my vehicle. Ready to blow a bitch to pieces, I dropped the gun to my side when I noticed it was Jon.

"Ken, I wasn't finished talking," he slurred. "The real reason, I fucked over you is because of that nigga you got pictures and strings of text messages in your phone from."

"What the fuck are you talking about? Did you follow me home?"

"C'mon now, you know I got people. That's beside the point. I'm here bout that nigga."

"Again, what the fuck are you talking about, Jon?"

"That nigga you going to spend the weekend with. Bitch, don't test my nuthafuckin' gangsta." He lunged toward me, then I drew down on him. He stopped dead in his tracks.

"Don't make me kill you, Jon. I don't want to do it but I will," I stood my ground firmly. "Now, what the fuck are you talking about?"

"You gone kill me for that nigga, Ken? Huh? After everything, we been through. When you went to the bathroom at the restaurant, your phone chimed and me being the nigga I am checked it. How fuckin' long y'all been seeing each other you slut ass bitch? Is that even my fuckin seed you carrying?"

"You got it all wrong. But since I'm not married to you anymore, I don't owe your pussy ass no explanation. Get the fuck off my lawn, Jon," I yelled.

Blowing out an exasperated breath, he charged into my direction. I cocked my semiautomatic weapon and pointed it directly at his head.

"Jon, please don't make me take you away from your children before our child gets to enjoy you. You are a great father but were a horrible husband so I will regretfully but happily take you out your misery."

He was pressing his luck, he walked toward me as I backed up to my door. Thankfully I had topnotch everything. My entry was fingerprint activated. I had the barrel to his head as he yelled, *do it*. But I knew he was in a drunken rage and I didn't want to kill him, God knows I didn't. To the left of me was a set of bushes, to the right of me was stones. He was inebriated to the one-hundredth power, so all I had to do was push him over.

"You are too fuckin weak to do it, bitch," he raised his hand, and I pushed him to my left into the bushes to avoid him hitting his head on the bricks to the right and dying anyway.

When I was sure he was down, I activated my thumbprint and entered my house. As soon as the door closed, I held the gun to my chest, slid down on the floor, and cried.

Bam! Bam! Bam!

"Open the fuckin door bitch, you're gonna pay for this shit."

Bam! Bam! Bam!

He beat on my door for at least five minutes. I heard the sirens in the distance. Apparently one of my neighbors heard the commotion. I peeped out the window as Jon jumped in his car skidding off, missing a cop car by inches.

The only thing on my mind was safety, I grabbed a few items, called Jawaine and told him what was going on and that I was catching the next red-eye to him because he was the only person, I felt safe with. Jon would definitely find me at my parents' house.

My phone beeped every two to three minutes with calls from Jon. I noticed that he left a voicemail with every call. I was not in a mood to talk or to listen. I got my shit and got out of there before the police came back for questioning, or he came back to kill me for what I'd done.

"Fuck him! Fuck you, Jon!" I yelled as I threw my toiletry and overnight bag into the trunk of my car and headed out.

Another call came through from him, but this time I sent it to voicemail before it made it there by ringing. Not soon after, Jawaine called with flight information, it was then I realized that I need to accept the facts. If I was honest with myself, my true love was held up in Milwaukee, Wisconsin. He was my best friend, and I could see that after all we'd been through, together and apart, he still loved me unconditionally.

Jawaine (We)

After paying the rent for the month at the Air BnB we'd stayed in previously, Kenleigh decided to move here to Milwaukee. It was day three, and she was all in, no chips left. Today we planned to go house hunting to find her and the baby the perfect home. Of course, it would be in my neighborhood. I couldn't believe Jon's foolish ass had taken it that far. First and foremost, why in the hell was he checking a woman's phone that he was no longer with?

"Hey bestie," Kenleigh greeted as I entered her temporary dwelling.

"Sup? It smells good in here."

"I just finished cooking dinner. I made lasagna."

"How long have you been up and moving around to be done making lasagna before 10 a.m.?"

"About five hours or so. I had a burst of energy this morning after I took a shower. I washed and folded my clothes, meal prepped for the next week, and cooked this fabulous meal for us to eat after we finish ripping and running these country ass streets." Kenleigh beamed with joy, and I refused to steal it from her.

"What time is the first showing?"

"10:30, and the next one is at 1:00. I can't believe I'm moving here."

"Why can't you believe it?"

"This is so different from the big city and the small country."

"So, it's a happy medium."

"Since you put it that way, I guess you're right."

Kenleigh and I had been spending a lot of time together, we still hadn't had sex, but we were more than likely prone to. I wasn't sure how much longer I could go without getting between those thighs. I'd been spending nights with her, spooning, and watching movies and shit; to say I wasn't playing the role, would be an understatement.

I was content with getting to know one another as adults before moving into sex or a relationship. After explaining to her my reservations about having sex with her, she clowned the hell out of me, telling me I sounded like a woman and shit, but I didn't give a fuck. I was a great man; women threw themselves at me day in and day out.

"Aye, you ready? I like to be early for everything."

"I know, Jawaine. You always have," she laughed. "You were the first crazy ass to be at the dances, the only one in the audience when the talent show started, hell you beat the ticketing booth to the basketball games."

"Oh, you funny, huh?" I laughed.

"No, I'm just saying," Kenleigh grabbed her oversized designer bag and headed for the door.

We rode two blocks east and three blocks north of where I lived to see the house on East Hampshire Avenue that Kenleigh was looking to buy. When I tell you it was a house, I mean it was a home. Five bedrooms, three baths, living room, den, kitchen, and separate dining room. It sat on 8,276 square feet of land and was near great schools. I had a gut feeling that even after visiting the other house, she'd still choose this one.

Ke had been here three days, and surprisingly, Joh hadn't been blowing her phone up. Not that I wanted him in her ear, her head, or her life, I was simply taken by his quietness in comparison to how she said he'd overreacted the night she'd jumped a plane and headed here.

Kenleigh had requested that I stopped referring to her as KeKe because it was a childhood nickname and didn't fit the woman she was today. I respected her wishes and was trying to find a name that suits her. Watching her phat ass walk through this house, I figured out what it could be.

"What about Vix?" I queried.

"Huh?"

"You said you wanted a nickname better than the old one and not one that someone else called you. What about Vix?"

"Why, Vix?" she quizzed.

"Short for Vixen. We both know you are a spitfire. The woman you are today will chew a nigga's ass up, spit him out, then feed him to the neighborhood's stray dogs."

The smile that spread over her face proved to me that she approved. However, the way she sashayed over to me, wrapped her arms around my waist and stared into my eyes spoke volumes. As I stared down at her, she pecked my lips and smiled.

By the time we covered the current residence from top to bottom, front to back, we had twenty minutes to get to the next property. While the second one was beautiful, it wasn't as breathtaking for her as the first one. If Kenleigh didn't get the first house, I'd be shocked. I wasn't gonna ruin the moment, but when we got back to the rental, I'd be questioning what this whole handholding, hugging, kissing, and spooning shit we engage in was about.

After we'd finished running our errands, we decided to walk around the mall. I picked up a few items for the baby and myself. I loved to smell good, so I picked up a few bottles of cologne. They were ones that were already in my collection but were almost empty.

When I pulled into the driveway, our phones chimed simultaneously. It was a rarity that my phone went off when I didn't work, but also alarming. To me, it was a sign of something bad. With both our heads facing our screens, we sighed loudly.

"It's my parents," I showed her my screen. They texted me from the family line, saying it was an emergency.

"Really? Mine was a message from Aunt Junie. She said the same thing."

We looked at each other in suspense. We questioned one another, trying to figure out if what it was, they were calling for was the same thing, or if it was a coincidental incident.

"Listen, neither of us knows what they want, the only way to find out is to call them. Correct?"

"Yeah, that's true. But what if it's uncle Bucky?"

"Why would you assume that?"

"I don't know. My nerves are bad right now for them to message us at the same time."

"Calm down," I rubbed her arm. "Let's head inside, put our things away, eat, and then call them back."

"Eat? Eat? Like seriously? Eat? Nah, I'm finna put these bags on the sofa and call my aunt back. You are trippin."

"I ain't trippin. I know for a fact that if it's something major, you won't eat. Your baby needs to eat. Please, eat first," I begged.

She stared at me all ornery like she wanted to contest, but I think she knew I wasn't going to allow her to do what she wanted. I was far from the Jawaine I was when she allowed me to refer to her as KeKe and if she tried me on some shit, she would find out.

"Thank you for listening hard head ass girl. Now, here you go, call Aunt Junie." I handed Kenleigh her phone before sitting next to her and rubbing her thigh.

"You think you running things but you ain't," she smiled.

She dialed Aunt Junie and waited as the lined trilled loudly through the earpiece. Honestly, her shit was so loud she should've had it on speakerphone.

"Hey baby, it's about time you called me back," Aunt Junie picked up.

"Hey Auntie, Jawaine and I were just pulling in, and he made me eat before I called."

"Good," Aunt Junie responded. "Where's Jawaine? I figured I'd deliver the news to the two of you at the same time, baby."

"Aunt Junie, you're scaring me. Is uncle Bucky okay? Are you okay? Are you guys dying?"

"No baby, we're both fine. You both need to hear this, put me on speaker," Aunt Junie said.

An uneasiness consumed my being. It wasn't until I heard her ask to be put on the speaker that I'd begun to worry. I could see the tears well in Kenleigh's eyes before either of us knew for sure what was happening. Grabbing her hand, I kissed it in an attempt to calm both her and me. With her barely being out of her second trimester, I didn't want or need her at risk for losing her child.

"Okay Aunt Junie, we're both here."

"Hey Peanut," Aunt Junie addressed me by a nickname she'd given me as a child.

"What's up beautiful? Is everything okay?"

"No, baby. I don't know how to tell either of you this. But I hate to have to do it by phone."

"Auntie just spit it out, please. You got my effin nerves on one hundred. Lord, just spit it out!"

The incredulous look I gave her must've willed an apology.

"I'm sorry, Aunt Junie. Although I didn't say the word, it was very disrespectful, and if I were in your presence, I would have lost my fronts."

"It's okay baby. A detective showed up at our door today asking for you Sugar Bear."

"For what? I'm cleaner than the board of health."

"They weren't looking for you about you, they were looking for you about Jonathan." The way she said that it made chills course through my body. Goosebumps were visible on both my forearms.

"What has Jon gotten himself into now? He can cut the freaking crap. I don't want to be with him, he'll never get another chance. Especially not after what he pulled the other night. He was like a manic, rabid, attack dog."

"Kenleigh, he's dead. Jon is dead." She wept.

"What?" we asked in unison.

Although I didn't like the dude, I never wished death on him. I wanted to whoop on him for what he'd put Kenleigh through, but I never imagined hearing what I was hearing. The nigga was a bad ass quarterback and a few years away from retirement. We were never friends, but we were on the same football team from seventh grade until our senior year of undergrad. I had brotherly love for him outside of the hate for stealing my girl.

"Yeah, apparently the night you left for Milwaukee; he led the police on a highspeed chase. He shot three cops and was killed by the partner of one of the fallen officers," Aunt Junie stammered through the story leaving us both shocked and confused.

"No, I don't believe that. I don't believe he did that because he called me several times and left voicemails each time."

"Has he reached out since, Sugar Bear?"

Kenleigh disconnected the line, not answering Aunt Junie. It wasn't meant to be disrespectful, from the look on her face, she was in utter disbelief.

"Baby, you okay?"

"No, I'm gonna call him. Jawaine, I gotta call him," she hit his contact, and it went to voicemail. She then dialed his number from her memory, it also went to voicemail. She left message after message until her phone chimed.

It had been confirmed, Kenleigh had shown me a few text messages from several of the football wives members sending their condolences. She tried calling Jon's cellphone again but to no avail. Enwrapping her into my arms, she laid her head on my chest and cried her eyes out. The only thing I knew how to do was be there for her.

Kenleigh (We)

It's been three weeks since I buried my ex-husband. Shockingly he'd listed me as the heir and beneficiary over everything he'd ever built for himself in life. From his luxury apartment to his shares in his partnerships. Being the person that I am, I sold everything I could, gave the condo to Justice, and turned the accounts over to a fiduciary to keep up with and divide into four accounts at twenty-five percent each, for his children.

LaShay said she didn't want anything. Nonetheless, I put Jon junior's money in trust fund for him. Glentrell, his daughter's mother, she was a different story. She had the nerve to be pissed because she wasn't listed on his obituary. Like, where the fuck they do that at? Not in any ghetto fabulous funeral in hell had I ever seen a baby mama named on a program. I didn't list myself, hell, and the ink was barely dry on our divorce papers.

The police tried to play the blame shit like I tried to kill him for the gain. They had the nerve to tell me I was a scorned wife trying to pay him back for the divorce that I had initiated. When I proved to them that my dividends could pay their whole department's salary and that I'd petitioned the court to dissipate our nuptials, the forgot they'd mentioned anything of the sorts.

"Vix, you ready?"

"Yeah, I guess I am."

"I'm excited and afraid at the same time."

"What are you afraid of, Jawaine?"

"What if they tell me I can't get no more of that good stuff?"

"Really? Boy, you silly as hell. You gon' be sliding in these guts til it's time to deliver. You got me messed up."

We'd finally got out of the friend zone, and that monster in his pants had tamed my ass. There was no way I was gonna allow him to keep me from the Alabama Black Snake. Yep, I sure did nickname his dick, and the name suits him well.

"Vix, what the hell you doing over there that got ya nipples pointing at me and ya thighs quivering?"

"Huh? Oh, nothing. You ready to go?"

"C'mon girl so we can get to the doctor. I got to work in a few hours."

I grabbed my things and headed to the car. I'd be closing on the home over on East Hampshire and was waiting for the finalization. Hopefully, in the near future, I'd be moving in. In all the weeks I'd been in Milwaukee, I still hadn't seen the inside of Jawaine's home, and I think I'm okay with it.

We'd decided to date each other exclusively and see where it goes. When he mentioned it, I understood his stance, and I respected his adult decision. The truth to the matter was, I was fresh out of a marriage to the only man I had ever slept with. Neither of us needed history to repeat itself.

Last week when I went to see my mom, Jawaine traveled with me. Trinh loved him, she said she reminded her of my father. That was a high honor being that my aunt and uncle talked about how great of a man he was. Speaking of which, I'd finally found the nerve to listen to the voicemails Jon left the night he died.

Voice *Message received May 10, 2019. Kenleigh, bitch if you don't pick this god damn phone up your ass is dead. If you think you gone leave me for that hoe ass nigga you and him gone pay! Message saved, next message.*

Voice Message received May 10, 2019. Kenleigh, please don't leave a nigga. I need you in my corner. Who's gonna put up with my shit, huh? Nobody Ken. You were the only bitch in the world that was willing to marry a nigga like me. Them other hoes were content with being the side bitch. I know you wasn't the only one, you was number one. I put you first, and you were too stupid and too selfish to accept the fact that a nigga cared enough to do the shit in front of your face so them hoes knew not to try to sneak behind my back to tell you what was going on- Message saved, next message.

Voice Message received May 10, 2019. Ken, I see you really done with a nigga, I'm out here running from the police, and you don't give a fuck. I know you don't cuz you tried to kill a nigga. I'm bout to take these bitches out, and I'm putting you on speaker so you can hear it all, bitch.

Car: Door ajar

Police: Drop your weapon

*Jon: FUCK YOU. *Pow*

Police: He opened fire, I need backup

Jon: Nah bitch my girl wanna hear you die to prove I give a fuck, c'mon out. You hear that Ken; you hear the sirens in the distance. Here comes the cavalry for your ass, c'mon out.

*Pow- Message saved, next message.

Message received, May 10, 2019, Oh Ken, I thought I lost you. *Pow Owww, these bitches shot me. *Pow I got one of these mufuckas Ken, *Pow *Pow, I got another one. I should've been a cop.

Police: Drop your fuckin weapon right now.

Jon: Nigga, you must be a ninja or some shit the way you snuck up on me. Get that fuckin gun off my head bitch. *scuffling noises *Pow *Pow Owwwww, nigga you shot me in my stomach. Ken, *gurgling noise. I'm sorry I treated you like shit, this is it for me, baby, I ain't gone make it. Tell all my kids I love them, including the one you in your belly, I know it's mine. I was mad. I love you, Ken. *loud labored breath and footsteps near the phone. Message saved.

The more I listened, the more I cried. I heard everything from him, to the car talking, to the police yelling, to the guns blazing, to his last breath. It was tragic.

"Kenleigh," Jawaine called out.

"Huh? What? Yeah, baby, what's up?"

"I don't know, you tell me. We were at the doctor's office for three minutes and you sitting there crying and unresponsive as you stare out the window. Should I be worried about you and the baby? Is there something you need to talk to me about?"

"Yes. No. Yes. I don't know. I don't want you to be mad at me."

"I'm confused."

"I listened to the messages Jon left. Even from the grave, he taunted me and told me how stupid and gullible I was. I'm scared to love again."

"I'm not asking you to rush into anything Vix. I'm only asking that you be sure of what you want. We will continue this friendship for as long as we both need. The one thing we have in common is that we both lost our spouse. I understand you need time."

"No, your spouse loved you, you don't feel my pain. Your spouse didn't beat your ass then laugh about it on her death bed. He did the shit intentionally. He called me during the shoot out with the police so he could haunt me the rest of my life."

"I can't argue with you, and I won't try. My wife loved me, and I loved her, but if this is what you are going to do, then whatever we are trying to form between us ain't gone work. We can't compare who loved who more, this will get us nowhere. Let's get this appointment over so I can go to work. I don't have time for these games you play."

Jawaine got out, walked around to the passenger's door, and opened it. He walked behind me as he always did, opened the door, then allowed me to sit while he signed me in. I don't know how I felt about his response. What I do know is, Trinh always says *hurt feelings, hurts feelings*.

My obstetrician is Bo's wife. She knew Jawaine and Biansha. At first, it was a little weird for me, but it is what it is, she came highly recommended and also had all five-star reviews on yelp and google.

The visit went well, everything was good with the baby. My blood pressure was elevated, but it wasn't critical, so Dr. Jones told me to take it easy. On the ride back to my crib, Jawaine didn't say much. I tried to make small talk, but he was giving me what I gave him. While he didn't ignore me completely, he replied directly. There wasn't any elaborating, straight yes, no, shoulder shrug, head shake, or head nod.

We pulled into my driveway, and he stopped directly behind my car, put his car in park, walked around to open my door, walked me to the door, kissed my head, and walked away. I knew he was pissed; he usually says *I love you Bestie* before he heads out for the day. I ain't sweating it though. He can act like a pussy all he wanted to. I didn't move here for him anyway, I moved here for me.

It's been three days, Jawaine was tripping. In the three days that he's been MIA, I've received five text messages. Three said, *Love you, bestie, good night* and two said *good morning beautiful.* If I didn't hear his voice today, I was gone pull up on his ass. And if he wasn't home, I was going to the precinct.

I was catching up on Games People Play, and the sex scene gave me a flashback of the first time Jawaine knocked the dust off my pussy.

"I'm gonna go home so you can have your space to grieve. I don't want to taint your process or be here to seemingly take advantage of you because we both know that's not what I do."

"No, Jawaine, please stay. I don't wanna be alone tonight. I need the company to keep my mind occupied. I mean yeah, we're divorced, but I still gave that man the best years of my life."

The moment I said that I realized how much it impacted him and what he was trying to do for me. I knew he meant well and that he wanted to show me the greater good, the value of twenty-four hours and why I was his Godsend, and he was mine. I blatantly held onto a falsehood, a dream, well truthfully a nightmare. My whole marriage was a farce, a sham, a dark tale.

"Well, I'mma sleep in the guestroom tonight, I'm a lil tired." Jawaine kissed my forehead and headed out.

An hour or so had passed, and I felt myself tiring out. My eyes were getting heavy, so I stood to my feet and dragged myself to the room to lay down. Just as I approached the room, Jawaine chose to sleep in. I heard a heavy snore. I thought it was weird that he liked to sleep with his door open rather than closed but who was I to judge him.

I peered in at him, and his dick was hanging out of his boxer hole. I struggled to close the distance of where I was planted and my bedroom in my temporary living situation. It was as if his member had me hypnotized. I turned my head to leave, and from the corner of my I, I noticed movement. His thick, chocolate rod stood to the occasion as if to say come and get it.

I approached him strategically in an effort not to wake him because I knew he'd contest. He kept saying it wasn't a good time, but when the fuck would it be. Licking my lips, I spat on my hand, grabbed his pole, and swallowed as much as I could. As I leaned over the side of the high bed, I worked his dick like the bottom bitch on a busy corner. Sucking and slurping, beating and kneading, I was determined to wake Jawaine up with the intent of him fucking me to sleep. I relaxed my jaws to take in the length, but the girth was another story. He grabbed my hair and lead me to victory

"Kenleigh, what the fuck you doing?" he grabbed me, steadying my pace to something less rough than what I was used to.

Don't misquote me. I was a pro at not using teeth. Sloppy top was what I knew. The faster I sucked, the faster the nut came, the faster I was done tasting other people's pussy. Jawaine ground his hips into my mouth, gagging me a little, it wasn't alarming or rough, so I welcomed it.

"Got damn it Kenleigh why the fuck you didn't let me initiate. Shit!" he grabbed my hair and pulled my head off of his dick. "Strip."

I looked at him dumbfoundedly, but his gaze was filled with lust, sexual tension, and fire. Doing as I was told, I stood in all my glory.

"Get in the bed." He growled.

Before I knew it, he was blowing my back out, and I was cursing his name. It was the best sex I ever had. Although he said I molested him, I know he enjoyed it because until three days ago we had sex almost every day.

"Ahhhhhh Shiiiiiiit!" I screamed as I pounded my middle and ring finger in and out of my wet pussy in a hooking motion. Jawaine had taught me how to touch my g spot. I threw my head back and lifted my leg up for more leverage. Within seconds, I was gushing like a fire hydrant.

"I'm gonna clean up and head to Jawaine's. What he's not going to do, is be selfish and childish. We all have bad days." I had to talk to myself because I didn't have friends.

"I don't know mom, I'm not into mending her. You told me all my life that there was two things you couldn't fix, and that was stupidity and people. What happens when she lashes out on me for something he did. I don't want to be anyone's punching bag. I understand grief, and I know personally the mass of the detrimental effect losing a spouse has on a person. It grabbed hold of me to a point I'd almost lost everything I'd worked for."

"Wanky, you came out of it. Give her some time baby, she'll come around."

"Mom, I'm thirty years old, I don't have time for games. It's been three days and she been on some good bullshit," I said to my mom, Huang.

"Listen Wanky and listen well. You had your time to yourself when you grieved your late wife and child. We didn't crowd you, nor did we rush you. It's not fair to her for you to act like grief has a time limit or a time to present itself. You asked her to be honest with you, and she was transparent at your request. Instead of you accepting and understanding her pain, you brushed it off and made it about you. I'm always the one to be honest with you, son. I'm never going to be your yes woman. Either you fix it or lose her again."

"I'm gonna head over to her place right now and make it right. Thank you, mom, for always keeping me in check and laying down the law when I need you to. Where's pop?"

"He done adopted a new habit since you've left. He goes across the track to pick boys up and train them in the gym. He has two now, a thirteen-year-old and a sixteen-year-old. They're good kids, just need a little guidance is all."

"Keep an eye on them, mom, you know pop is kindhearted and everybody ain't good," I headed to the door to go apologize to my best friend.

I pulled the door open just as Kenleigh raised her hand to ring the doorbell. She smiled timidly, and I gave her a half-grin.

"What's up Vix?" I quizzed like I wasn't headed her way. "I'll call you back. Love you Piggy," I said to my mom.

I guess we were having a stare off to see who'd speak first. I was a man, and I'd told mom that I was going to make it right, so there was no sense in standing here acting childish.

"Come in," I stood to the side to allow her entry to my home for the first time.

All reservations of allowing Kenleigh in my house went out the window. Honestly, I didn't think twice about not letting her in, when I laid my eyes on her, I forgot how to breathe. Kenleigh looked around my abode and took in her surroundings. Here I was pissed about her listening to her recently pulseless ex-husband's voicemail, but I still had pictures of my deceased wife in every room of my home except the bathroom, and she'd been gone for some years.

What a fuckin' double standard. How dare I be such a hypocrite? It wasn't fair of me to secretly judge her for her feelings nor her actions.

"I apologize for how I reacted to your admission. I had no reason to behave the way I did. I'm supposed to keep you safe from harm, not throw you to the wolves for feeling a certain way. It's taken me years to come to terms with my wife being slain and the fact that she's never coming back scared the hell out of me. Look around, I tried keeping her alive in my head and in my heart by leaving everything the way it once was."

"Jawaine, I don't know how to feel. I don't know if I should be sad, happy, or indifferent because of how bad things were between us. He was cruel to me, but I loved him. I thought I could fix him. Unfortunately, I found out the hard way that I couldn't fix him because he'd been broken far too long."

"I'm sorry you went through such a hard time, and I give you my deepest condolences. I know how it feels to have loved and lost, Lord knows I do. We are in similar situations; I watched my wife get taken away, and you listened to your ex-husband take his last breath. I don't know how to help you other than allowing you time to grieve and accept the loss. Until you are ready, I'm willing to be the friend you need, the companion you want, and the chef your stomach craves."

"What about the sex I need to blow my back out?" she smiled devilishly.

"Nope, you ain't gone be using me to pipe you down. That's out right there," I half grinned.

"But I need you bad like a heartbeat, badder than the air I breathe." Kenleigh laughed at her failed attempt to sing Jazmine Sullivan's song. She sounded like a wet cat.

"First things first, we need to set the ground rules."

"I thought we'd already established those?" Kenleigh looked confused.

"Well we did, that was before sex though. After I blew that back out, shit changed. Ha. Ha. Ha."

"So," Kenleigh waited.

"We can't have sex in this house until it's redecorated. I won't disrespect you or my late wife by making love, having sex, or fucking the shit out of you on every piece of furniture that I had her on. We are dating until we are both ready for commitment. There will be an open floor between us, transparency when it comes to grief. It hits different because we know what each other is experiencing. If we know we don't wanna be bothered, we say hey, not tonight." I breathed.

"Is that dating exclusively, or is it ok that I get that wood from someone else when you holding out on me?"

"Hey, it is what it is. As long as when you see me in public with my boo, you don't act a damn fool. I like conversation, public displays of affection, and doing shit that doesn't require being laid up stuffing holes with my pole. So, if you good, I'm good." I half smiled to see where she'd take it.

"Oh, okay. That's what we doing, Jawaine?"

"Nah, that's what you doing. Give my pussy to someone else and see don't I fuck both of y'all up."

I grabbed the back of her head and pulled her to me. Jamming my tongue down her throat, I grabbed a handful of her phat ass and pulled her into my hard erection, then ground her. Her stomach was growing like a weed. I wanted some of the good stuff.

"Can we go? I need to get in my sweet spot."

"Oh, it's we, huh?"

"Yeah girl, you trippin?" I asked. "It's she," I kissed her shoulder. "Plus, he," I thumbed my chest. "Equals we." I slid my hands up her arms, held her face, then kissed her again. "Now let's go before I change my mind."

"Mom, I love you so much. We will definitely visit you after the baby is born, you don't have to worry your head about that." Kenleigh spoke to her mom on the phone as we drove from the airport to visit our parents. It was almost Independence Day, and we both were craving home. Kenleigh was due August 10, so we decided to get our last travel out before the baby.

While we were still living in separate quarters, and still friends with benefits, we were falling in love slowly but surely. While I was content with the way things were between us, I was not complacent. I don't share well because I am an only child. Therefore, I must admit I suffer from two things… having everything to myself and a minor case of affluenza.

We pulled up into the cul-de-sac and parked onside the curb. We sat for a moment to allow time for Kenleigh to bring her call to a close. After a few minutes, I got out and opened her door for her. Walking up to the porch, I took notice of the changes that Uncle Bucky had made to the house, they were nice. He finally got the all-weather screens for the door and windows. Although his home was run by automatic air conditioner and heat, those screens will keep it temperate.

"Sugar Bear!" Aunt Junie yelled, pulling her into a hug.

She stepped back admiring Kenleigh's protruding belly. It was a beautiful sight to see. I'd missed this trimester of Ninny's pregnancy but look at God, He'd blessed us to fall in each other's laps as we needed to at the time we needed. They say He's an on-time God and His time, not ours. When I was younger, I didn't get the gist of it, but as a man, I fully understood and appreciated its true meaning.

"Hey Peanut," Aunt Junie spoke as I hugged her neck and kissed her head.

"Heeey nah, Sugar Bear!" Uncle Bucky greeted Kenleigh with a huge smile and a kiss on the cheek. Uncle Bucky was my second dad, I had a feeling he was about to be on some shit.

"What's up, son?" he jabbed me in the side, and I really wanted to knock him on his ass. Well, I wanted to, but that didn't mean if I tried I would be able to. Between him and Bao, my dad, I learned everything I know.

"What's up, Unc? Bruh, your knuckles are hard. Why you gotta be punching on me though?" I laughed but wasn't shit funny.

"It smells good in here Auntie, what you cooked?"

"Sugar Bear, can you smell through the phone?"

"Yes, sir, I sure can. It's a pregnant woman's superpower."

The doorbell rang while we all sat at the table. Aunt Junie had whole catfish, baked macaroni, cornbread, and mustard greens. She'd also made a tres leches cake. It was a Hispanic thing, but we all loved it.

My parents walked in, looking aged. It worried me because I thought when I moved out, they would be less stressed. As they rounded the corner so did two teenaged boys, one white, he was tall and skinny and one black, not tall at all.

Mom went to sit, and one of them pulled her chair out for her. The gesture caused me to smile. I knew it was all my dad, he'd always catered to mom. We sat and talked, I got to know the boys and one of them told me something that just chapped my ass. He said, he'd never wanted to fall in love with anyone because love hated him, beat him, and abandoned him. Love had dealt him a bad hand, and since love had never done anything good for him, he was over it already.

Ultimately, we stayed in Alabama for a week. I went by to visit Ninny's family. We spoke often, so I felt it necessary to see them while I was there. Vix understood and respected my stance, so I appreciated her for it. When we got back to Milwaukee, she signed the deeds on her new home, she said she wasn't looking to build her credit, and she was sure about the house, so she paid it outright, no strings attached.

We shopped for furniture for both our homes, me picking all blacks and greys. I'd ended up donating all my furniture to St. Vincent De Paul and giving Ninny and the baby's stuff to women and children shelter. It wasn't as hard to part ways with that I'd assumed. It was finally time to get back to being me after such a grave loss. Three weeks had passed and it was time for Kenleigh to give birth. Uncle Bucky and Aunt Junie had come to stay with her for the six weeks of recovery. She'd given birth to a beautiful baby girl. She weighed seven pounds, fourteen ounces and was twenty-one inches long. Kenleigh decided to name her Trinh Taviana Freeman-Li. I called her TT and she was and forever will be my princess.

In all that we've encountered in our lives and all that we've accomplished, I'm glad we've made it here. Thank you, God, we're moving on your time, not ours.

Epilogue

(Jawaine's Perspective)

Two Years Later...

Not in a million years would I have imagined losing my wife and unborn child to a murderer. My life was put on hold for a long time because I was afraid to live and terrified of love. When I was younger, I thought for sure the girl of my dreams was my childhood crush, Kenleigh Nguyen-Peters. God set it up to where we both went our separate ways and learned how to live on our own, in order for us to grow into the people we are today.

In a perfect world, Kenleigh would have fallen in love with me in junior high school, married me, and had my children right out of college like any other childhood sweethearts did. Unfortunately, we both had to experience life for us to find out who we were destined to be as individuals and predestined to be as adults. The outcome, thus far, has been sweet.

It was that fateful night at the Fairmont Olympic Hotel in Seattle, Washington that closed the gap on the love that had manifested itself within us at the tender ages of eight years old. A love that no one, but God, knew existed… and our parents, of course.

I stood back and watched in shock and disbelief, while Aunt Junie wiped the sweat from Kenleigh's forehead, and my mom held her hand as she practiced her breathing exercises. We'd attended child birthing classes when she was pregnant with Trinh, but this time, we were ready. We'd experienced the gift of life a little under two years ago and my God, my little TT was my world.

It was too bad her father, Jonathan never got the chance to see the beautiful child he'd helped to create. I thought it was pretty dope that she named baby girl after her mother and allowed me to give her my last name. Little Miss Trinh Freeman-Li, she was as beautiful as her mother was and I was as proud as my parents were. I now knew what they felt watching me grow.

"Get this baby out of me please!" Kenleigh screamed to the top of her lungs.

"It's gonna be okay Sugar Bear," Aunt Junie continued to dab her forehead with the wet towel.

"Wanky, come hold her hand for a few minutes so I can use the restroom," my mom suggested.

When I approached, my mother pried her had from Kenleigh's grip and shook it back to life. Apparently, she'd been squeezing the shit out of mom's hand. As she headed to the door, my dad followed her. The look in his eyes told me he was headed to the cafeteria, with his hungry ass. I had to laugh at my thoughts, I too was a little famished myself.

"What's so damn funny, you ain't being ripped from the rooter to the tooter. Keep acting up, and I'm gonna put you, ooooouch!" her rant was cut short by a contraction.

"Vix, it's gonna be okay baby. We're almost to the finish line."

"Easy for you to say, you don't have electric shockwaves traveling through your vagina."

I smirked at her; I knew she was in a lot of pain because she chose to go natural again. With TT, she was excited enough to make it through the pain without drugs. At this point, I want to suggest an epidural before it's too late to have it. Her ass is mean as shit this time around.

I held her hand and gazed into her beautiful orbs. I was so nervous about tonight. Kenleigh and I were still only dating each other, we still lived in separate quarters, and although we always said we loved one another, neither of us has said that we were in love with each other.

"I don't like you laughing at me while I'm going through this Jawaine, it's not funny."

"I'm not laughing at you Vix, I'm admiring you. I think you are so beautiful and vulnerable and strong. I'm smirking because you're amazing. You're superwoman in my eyes."

"Awwwwe!" my mom and Aunt Junie sang in unison.

When I witnessed the tears spring from Kenleigh's eyes, I had to keep my own orbs from watering up. I had been thinking about us and where to take this thing between us would go. We're having a baby and are still in the friend zone, this isn't how either of our parents had raised us.

I held her hand and leaned in to kiss her lips, she had snot and tears over her face, but I didn't care. I loved her; I truly loved the woman that was due to give birth to my child at any point today.

Kenleigh panted, then screamed when we broke our kiss. It scared the living shit out of me. "What happened?" I quizzed.

"I don't know, but my coochie feels like it's splitting open, and I need to get up because I gotta drop the kids off at the pool."

"Drop the kids off at the pool? What kids?" my dad asked as he and my mom re-entered the room.

"Oh no, oh no," Aunt Junie said.

She hit the nurses light to get the attention of the nurses, but whoever was monitoring her must've been aware. They'd busted into the room, asked everyone to stand back so they could perform a pelvic exam.

"She's crowning... You're crowning. I need you to breathe and try not to push ok." She said to Kenleigh.

Pressing the button on the little walkie talkie thing on her scrub top, she spoke into it. "Call Dr. Jones."

"Vocera, calling Doctor Jones." The walkie talkie responded.

"Dr. Jones," Bo's wife's voice resounded from the speaker.

"Ms. Peters will be having a baby soon, she's crowning."

"I'm on my way. Get her prepped for delivery."

"Yes, ma'am," the nurse responded. "Who's all staying for the delivery?"

"Me," I spoke.

"Me," Aunt Junie said.

"Me," my mom smiled.

My pop and Uncle Bucky looked at each other, "Not us," they belted out and headed toward the door with TT.

The nurse had us scrub in and don personal protective equipment. She told us it was to avoid outside germs. After a long drawn out explanation and instructions that me and Aunt Junie was aware of, Dr. Jones busted in the door.

"I hear we're ready to have a baby. It's ready, I'm ready, are you guys ready?" Dr. Jones rambled off, filled with excitement.

After fifteen minutes of pushing, screaming, and damming us all to hell, Kenleigh gave birth to our baby.

"It's a girl, ladies, and gentlemen. Jawaine, c'mon over and cut the cord." Dr. Jones suggested, and I did.

They showed the baby to us, then the nurses took her over to the warmer to clean her up, weigh her, and then placed her on Kenleigh's chest. Uncle Bucky and pop came in with TT in their arms.

"Ooooh, baybeeee!" she babbled when she saw her baby sister.

Everyone was standing around in admiration of Kenleigh, I was sweating bullets. I'd already spoken with my pop and Uncle Bucky about the plans that were about to be a reality. I stood to my feet, took the baby from Kenleigh, and handed her to Aunt Junie, then sat TT on the bed next to Kenleigh.

"Kenleigh and TT, I was in a very dark place. It took me a very long time to see the light of day again and honestly even that light was still dim. Kenleigh, the night you asked me for my autograph at the convention, you lifted a dead weight from my shoulder. You've given me a family and will to live, and for that, I wanna thank you.

I told you that I'd always be here for you and that's a promise. I don't ever want you to have to fend for yourself or take care of our babies alone. I know that you are both emotionally and financially stable enough to provide, but I want to be your strength, your provider, your good mornings, and your great nights. I would love to be at every turn of you and our kids' lives. I wanna see every first step, missing tooth, scraped knee, bike fall, and graduation.

I wanna see your hair turn gray, watch you grow old, and sit in the swing on our porch with our grandchildren. I have loved you my whole life Kenleigh Nguyen-Peters, and here I stand in the presence of every important person in our lives, I want to admit to you before them and before God that I am absolutely in love with you."

"I ya you hoo dayee," TT blurted out, causing everyone to laugh.

Turning to TT, I smiled at her, then kissed her head and continued.

"I know we said we were content with us the way things were, but my heart sn't going to allow me to go into the next year without you at least being my fiancé. I said all of this to ask you," I got down on one knee and grabbed her hand. "I love you more than life, always have and always will. Will you do the honors and make my life complete? Kenleigh Nguyen-Peters, will you marry me?"

With tears in her eyes and trembling hands, she looked around as I stared at her waiting for an answer. I don't think I heard my pop or Uncle Bucky breath the whole time. She wiped her face with the sleeve of her gown and smiled down at me. I was as nervous as a Saturday night whore in a church on a Sunday morning.

"Why are you sweating, baby? You should already know the answer to your question. You also came in my life during my darkest days, we won't get into the details of that. However, you held me down through loss and life. With all our years and all of the obstacles set in our paths, we found each other. I will love you beyond infinity… Yes, Detective Jawaine Franklin-Li, I will marry you."

I slid the rock on her hand and kissed her like I would never see her again.

"Okay, okay that's why we're here now. Kissing," Uncle Bucky said.

We all laughed. He'd always told us that kissing would get Kenleigh pregnant, so he didn't want us kissing. So, there was an insider we all understood. I turned to TT, kissed her cheek, then grabbed her hand.

"Trinh, as your father and the man responsible for your well being, I want to ask for your permission to be your dad forever. Can I be your dad forever, TT?"

"Yes, dayee, I ya you!" she responded, and everyone laughed as I placed an infinity necklace around her neck. It had both our names engraved in the loops. It may be cheesy, but I thought it was special.

We all spent a few weeks together. Our parents stayed around until Kenleigh had fully recovered. During the weeks, we'd decided to move in together. I packed my things and relocated into Kenleigh's home being that there were so many memories in mine of me and my late wife. Her home was way bigger than mine, so we would have fun filling the home with more children. She'd already made it clear, she wanted six children, and I had no problem giving her more.

As we loaded the car with our parents' bags, Aunt Junie and my mother called us into the family room to show us what they'd been working on in there and why we'd been denied entry. On the far wall was a sheet pinned covering something.

"Please, stand back because we don't know if the pins will pop off and hit anyone," mom said. She and Auntie laughed, but we were looking at one another like what the hell.

"One, two, three," Auntie called out.

When they pulled the cover, three hand-painted art pieces were revealed. One to the left was of Kenleigh, above the frame on the wall was the word *She*. One in the middle was of me, and above that frame on the wall was the word *He*. To the right of that was a picture of me, Kenleigh, and the kids. Above that was the word *We*.

While we were smiling and speechless, the math symbols between each painting had us confused. We had no earthly idea what the hell it symbolized. With all the education between us, you'd think we would've been quick on our feet.

"This is beautiful ladies, but what is the pictorial representation of this, honey? What does this mean?" my dad asked.

Mom let out a sigh. Obviously frustrated because she'd realized none of understood the expression. Aunt Junie looked pissed.

"It's the equation of love people," Aunt Junie spoke.

"She Plus He Equals We."

The End

CPSIA information can be obtained
at www.ICGtesting.com
Printed in the USA
LVHW031717280120
645065LV00004B/671